"You're a cheat and a liar. I hate you!"

Vicky stared at Jay defiantly, and then her hand rose and slapped him hard across his cheek. "You're the most despicable man I've ever met."

"Isn't that rather like the pot calling the kettle black?" Jay replied.

"If you're referring to George—" she said.

"And Barry, and no doubt a few others I don't know about." A sneer curled his lips. "And you have the nerve to call me a cheat and a liar!" He stepped closer again, and his eyes ranged slowly over her. Passion had enlarged the irises of his eyes, and his jaw moved in a tense, uncontrolled manner.

"There's only one thing a girl like you understands," he said thickly, and giving her no chance to escape, he pulled her close and pressed his mouth on hers.

D0043240

Kay Clifford is a British writer who has been writing for the Harlequin Romance line for the past few years. Readers will welcome her newest, lightly sophisticated romance.

Recipe for Love
Kay Clifford

Harlequin Books

TORONTO • NEW YORK • LONDON
AMSTERDAM • PARIS • SYDNEY • HAMBURG
STOCKHOLM • ATHENS • TOKYO • MILAN

Original hardcover edition published in 1986
by Mills & Boon Limited

ISBN 0-373-02912-8

Harlequin Romance first edition June 1988

CHAPTER ONE

CLAUDINE had shown Vicky the letter first thing that morning, but she had been too busy to give it more than a passing glance. Now, over mid-morning coffee in Claudine's study, she was able to absorb it at leisure.

'I am head of a large company and wish to attend your summer cookery session,' she read. 'I cannot guarantee to attend every class, and owing to this I shall require extra lessons to make up for those I miss. I am prepared to pay well for the privilege, and will be happy to double your normal fees.'

The signature below was an almost illegible scrawl, though the typed name, J. P. Duncan, was quite clear, as was the cheque which fluttered to the table.

'What do you think?' Claudine Beauclare asked in a voice that still held strong traces of a French accent, in spite of its owner having lived in England for the past thirty-eight years. 'Shall we take her or not?'

'How can we refuse?' Vicky answered. 'It's a fantastic offer. The woman's obviously some high-powered executive with a bigger expense account than sense! But in any case, as we're a cookery school, I think we should be allowed the licence of taking a baker's dozen!'

Claudine chuckled. 'We'll have to make it quite clear to Ms Duncan we're making an exception for her because of her circumstances.'

'You mean because of ours! That extra seventeen hundred pounds will pay off the balance owing on the new ovens!'

'Do you think Wilson will have finished decorating the Mrs Beeton room by Tuesday?' the Frenchwoman asked, referring to the school caretaker. 'It's the largest and brightest, and for the money J P Duncan's prepared to pay, I think she's entitled to the best!'

Vicky pushed a long strand of black hair away from her forehead. 'I've already spoken to Wilson and he'll work over the weekend if need be.'

Claudine sighed. 'How could I ever manage without you, *ma chère*? You know what I'm thinking almost before I do!'

'I'll put that theory to the test right now by agreeing to give this woman the extra tuition she's asked for. As you say, she's entitled to the best—and after you, that's me! Dr Farley told me your blood pressure's up again, and he wants me to make sure you don't overdo things.'

'As if I could with you around.' Light blue eyes rested affectionately on Vicky. 'But I feel very guilty about asking you. As it is, you hardly find time to see Barry, and——'

'You didn't ask me, I volunteered,' Vicky cut in firmly. 'Now let's go through the schedules again. I want to see if I can rearrange a couple of the classes.'

It was nearly twelve-thirty by the time Vicky left the study to type out the notes she had made, as well as an acceptance letter to Ms Duncan. As she crossed the main hall and climbed the back staircase to the staff wing, she reflected ruefully on the extra work she had let herself in for. Barry would not be pleased. They saw little enough of each other as it was, and he had remarked on it at the weekend.

'You're more elusive than Garbo!' he had complained. 'Why doesn't Claudine take on more staff, instead of working you so hard? Surely she can afford it?'

'Unfortunately she can't. Our teacher-pupil ratio is very high, and she barely makes ends meet because of it.'

Barry had looked surprised. 'If she doesn't make much with the school full to capacity, what would happen if she was suddenly hit by the recession?'

'That's extremely unlikely. We have a waiting list long enough to fill another school.'

'In that case you ought to try to cram in a few more students.'

'That's not Claudine's way,' said Vicky. 'It's taken her years to build Beauclare's reputation as the finest cookery school in the country, and it's only by keeping up the standard that she can maintain her reputation.'

'She still has to find a way to make the school profitable,' Barry insisted.

'That's why we're running summer courses. They're mainly patronised by older women, who have the time and money to combine a holiday in a beautiful house with learning to cook.'

'And meanwhile, you're her willing slave!'

'Yes,' Vicky said with unusual sharpness. 'And I'd work twice as hard for her if need be—after all she's done for Felice and me!'

Claudine's parents had been killed in the war, and she had escaped to England, where she had become a school friend of Vicky's mother. When Vicky's parents had died in a car crash, she had immediately assumed care of ten-year-old Vicky and her adopted sister, Felice, a gesture Vicky would never cease to appreciate.

Vicky thought of this now, as she finished typing an acceptance to Ms Duncan, and wished Barry were more understanding of her feelings for the French-woman. He was calling for her in half an hour to take her to lunch, and because she knew he hated to be kept waiting, she rushed to get ready.

Standing in front of her somewhat lack-lustre wardrobe, she debated what to wear. As Claudine's deputy, she received a generous salary, but a good deal of it went on helping her sister Felice to keep out of debt. An aspiring actress, she was best known for her appearances in the gossip columns! Vicky did not approve of her sister's waywardness, but nevertheless she felt reponsible for her, and when Felice had forwarded a curt letter from her bank manager, threatening action unless her overdraft was reduced, Vicky had accepted responsibility for it, against Claudine's advice. Which was why, for the second year running, she had had to cancel her summer holiday and work on at the school.

It would have to be the turquoise and white silk print again, she finally decided. Barry liked it, and at least it did not have the serviceable air of most of her other dresses. Bought in a moment of frivolity, with a bonus Claudine had pressed on her, it accentuated her dramatic colouring of creamy skin, jet-black hair—thick and shiny and worn away from her face—and wide-apart, sapphire-blue eyes. They were large and slanted at the corners, and gave her a faintly provocative look, completely at variance with her blunt and practical disposition. Nature had been equally kind to the rest of her features: tip-tilted nose, generously wide mouth, with a full, softly curved lower lip, and high cheekbones that threw her eyes into prominence, so that even with the minimum of make-up she still glowed with life.

Taller than average, five-feet-six without shoes, she was so slender in build that she appeared smaller, but, conscious of her height, she carefully chose low-heeled shoes, that did little to flatter her long, shapely legs. Her clothes too were generally chosen to detract rather than attract, and more often than not, her perfectly proportioned figure was hidden beneath shapeless aprons. It would never do to look too glamorous in front of parents. But there was no way of disguising the fact that at twenty-four she was little older than some of her pupils. No need either, as, in spite of her youth, she radiated an air of self-confidence and assurance that befitted her role of deputy head-cook. But she did not have to worry about her image now, and she was lavish with mascara and lipstick.

Barry was waiting for her in the drawing-room that led off from the main hall. The view he was admiring from one of the long windows was quite breathtaking, and Vicky never failed to be moved by it herself: sun-drenched green lawns leading down to a miniature lake, upon whose glittering surface a pair of swans glided serenely beneath overhanging willows. Maintaining the house as a Georgian gem contributed to the high cost of running Beauclare's, but Vicky could understand Claudine's obsession with it. It took the place of husband and family.

'On time as usual.' Barry turned and kissed her lightly on the mouth, before leading her out to his car.

A couple of inches taller than Vicky, he was a personable-looking young man, with fairish hair and light brown eyes. He had an easy charm and a good sense of humour, something he often needed in his profession as a vet. They had met nearly a year ago at a party, and had dated constantly since. But Vicky was uncertain of her feelings, and wondered if it would be kinder not to monopolise his time. By doing so, she was encouraging him to believe she felt more than she did.

'Want to do any shopping after lunch?' he asked, cutting into her thoughts as the car purred down the driveway. 'I've a call to make at Lowson's farm, and I'll be about an hour.'

'I want to bank a cheque, but that's all,' she replied. 'I don't mind browsing around for a while, though, even if I can only afford to window-shop!'

'You're mad to keep paying off Felice's debts,' he said, reiterating Claudine's sentiments. 'She's been spoiled rotten, and you shouldn't go on encouraging her to live beyond her means. You're usually so practical!'

'How dreadfully dull that sounds,' Vicky laughed. 'But I assure you I'd like nothing better than to be madly extravagant!'

Barry swung into the car park of the Jolly Miller restaurant, on the outskirts of the market town of Granton, and they were soon seated at a table overlooking the river.

'How about an aperitif before we order?' he asked, and looked surprised when she agreed. 'You must have had a tough morning! It's the first time I've known you accept a drink other than wine.'

'It's always hectic before we re-open.'

'And it will be even worse when you have!'

'You can always come and see me during classes,' she grinned. 'You might even learn to boil yourself an egg!'

'I wouldn't dream of it!' he exclaimed in mock

horror. 'My mother taught me that a woman's place is in the kitchen, and a man's by the hearth!'

By the time Barry dropped her home, after a visit to the local cinema, it was nearly eleven-thirty. His goodnight embrace told her he would have liked to prolong the evening still further, but she yawned ostentatiously, and he took the hint.

'See you on Saturday as usual?' he asked.

'Sure.'

Vicky waited on the stone step until his tail lights disappeared, then made her way across the hall to the main kitchen. She was making herself a hot drink when the door swung open and Claudine came in, her salt-and-pepper grey hair neatly tucked into a blue hairnet that matched her quilted dressing-gown.

'Felice phoned this evening,' said Claudine. 'She's coming down next week to help out.'

Vicky looked surprised. 'I thought she'd been offered a part in a TV commercial?'

'Like most of her jobs, this one seems to have vanished into thin air. That's why she rang—she wanted more money from you. I told her you didn't have any, and that she should stop scrounging, so she said she'd come down here and earn her keep.'

'She must be hard up,' commented Vicky drily.

'Well, I refuse to let you be put upon again—and *I* certainly won't let her have any more to squander. I——' Claudine stopped abruptly, realising she had made a *faux pas*.

'What do you mean, *you* won't let her have any more?' asked Vicky slowly. 'Don't tell me she's been borrowing from you as well?'

'Only a few hundred pounds—and it wasn't a loan. I gave it to her for drama classes,' said Claudine defensively.

Vicky could not help smiling. 'And you're the one telling *me* not to be a soft touch!'

'At least I can afford it more than you.' Claudine tried to cover her mistake by sounding severe. But she couldn't sustain it, and smiled sheepishly. 'I suppose she blew the lot on clothes, as usual.'

'Probably,' Vicky agreed. 'Somehow I can't see her sticking it here for long. She'll be bored to death! Anyway, what about Chris? Did she mention him?'

'They've had a row and he's gone to cool off at his parents' villa at Cap d'Antibes. I thought with Joan Bryan away, Felice could organise the leisure activities.'

'Well, she can't take a cookery class,' commented Vicky drily. 'Take away her tin opener, and she'd starve!'

'Only because she's lazy,' Claudine observed. 'She's an extremely capable girl, but we've spoilt her and allowed her to get away with it.'

Later that night, lying in bed, Vicky tried to imagine Felice in the role of general dogsbody. Being at the beck and call of the well-heeled matrons who attended the summer seminars was hardly her forte, and she couldn't see her sister, however broke, sticking the job for long. Her main ambition was to find a rich husband, an attitude alien to Vicky herself, though it didn't alter the affection she felt for her sister. Deliberately, she never used the word love. The emotion Felice aroused had never been that deep, though it had nothing to do with the fact that their relationship was not a blood one. Claudine was not a blood aunt, yet she loved her more than if she had been.

Undoubtedly Claudine reciprocated her feelings, and had made it clear she saw Vicky as her successor.

Now, in the autumn of her life, a deep, consuming love had come to Claudine, though she still refused all George's blandishments to marry him, aware that divorce could endanger his High Court appointment and the knighthood that would accompany it. Because of this, she was prepared to continue in her role as 'other woman' for the rest of her days.

George, at her insistence, had promised to use his visit to the Far East as a cooling-off period, which would enable him to think things over. But he had made it plain before he left that there was nothing *to* think over. After a sterile and loveless marriage, where his wife's youthful beauty had bewitched him into believing there was some kind of depth behind it, he had found true happiness for the first time, and was prepared to make whatever sacrifices were necessary to bring it to fruition.

If the best did happen—and as far as Vicky was concerned, that meant their marriage—she had no need to worry about her own future, even if the school was closed down. She had already refused a couple of offers of finance for a restaurant with herself as cook/patronne, and they had both been left open for the foreseeable future.

It was a pity Claudine could not be persuaded to run a restaurant from the house, but when the school had shown a loss for the first time, she had plumped for the summer seminars as a solution to the problem.

'People would only compare me to my father,' she had given as the reason. 'And I'm not in his class.'

Ms Duncan's cheque would be icing on the gingerbread this summer, and Vicky wondered what the woman was like. Probably a high-powered executive used to steamrollering her subordinates as a way of proving that she was as good at her job as any man. There was no doubt it was flattering to know she had chosen to come to this school in preference to any other, regardless of cost, but she could well be a difficult woman to teach. Her letter had made it clear she expected private lessons for any that she missed due to company meetings, and Vicky acknowledged that the burden of this would fall on herself.

Sighing, she thumped her pillow into a more comfortable position, and accepted that she was going to have little chance of relaxing, or taking advantage of the holiday atmosphere of the seminar. Tennis, swimming and sunbathing would have to wait for another few weeks, at least.

CHAPTER TWO

FELICE arrived, complete with four large suitcases, on the following Sunday, stepping out of a chauffeur-driven Mercedes—loaned by one of her exes with whom she had remained on friendly terms—looking more like a rich student than one of the staff. Her white linen jacket and skirt were obviously expensive, as was the matching see-through silk shirt. The outfit showed off her copper-red hair to perfection—helped along by Miss Clairol, rather than entirely due to Mother Nature, although she would have been eye-catching anyway. Five-feet-two and slender—though well-endowed in the places that mattered—she was a perfect chocolate-box beauty: creamy complexion, straight nose, large green eyes, and a rosebud mouth, painted fuller than it really was.

Seeing her after an absence of several months convinced Vicky that there was more to Felice's decision to come here than met the eye. Two months in comparative isolation, with only the locals to break the monotony, would bore her to tears. Could she be running away from something? It seemed a possible explanation—but from what? She was not the type of girl who took her love affairs to heart, so it was unlikely to be Chris Ryder's exit from her life.

'Come and help me unpack,' Felice's voice cut across Vicky's thoughts. 'I've loads to tell you!'

She tucked her arm companionably in Vicky's, and moved towards the back staircase, above which the staff bedrooms and their own were situated.

15

'Claudine told me about you and Chris. I'm sorry.'

'Don't be,' said Felice. 'You were right about him all along. Do you know he wanted me to make a pornographic film for a friend of his?'

'And he professed to be in love with you!'

Felice shrugged. 'Love is a cheap word to men like Chris.'

'You're taking it very philosophically, considering you were hoping he'd ask you to marry him.'

'Only because I've bigger and better fish to fry,' she answered mysteriously, and began to unpack.

'If you've got someone else, I'm surprised you're willing to leave him in London and come down here,' remarked Vicky curiously.

'He won't be in London after tomorrow.'

'Where will he be?'

'On a business trip—but I'm hoping it'll turn out to be a pleasure as well!'

When Felice talked in riddles she could be exasperating. 'You've obviously no intention of explaining what you mean, so I won't ask,' said Vicky.

'You'll find out soon enough, and you'll be green with envy.'

'I doubt it. We've never liked the same men— fortunately!'

Felice smiled. 'How *is* Barry, by the way? Still making a fortune examining cows' udders?'

'Moo, moo!'

'I guess I deserved that,' said Felice contritely. 'As it happens, I like Barry. You could do a lot worse.'

'I know—and I tell myself that whenever I think he's about to pluck up the courage to propose.'

'Still hoping for love *and* marriage?' Felice sounded amused.

'Aren't you?'

The younger girl appeared to give the question consideration. 'I suppose so—but most of the men I meet aren't particularly lovable!'

'Then how can you go to bed with them?'

'I didn't say they weren't fanciable.'

'I know I'm old-fashioned, but to me they're one and the same thing,' said Vicky.

'Old-fashioned?' Felice expostulated. 'You're positively archaic! You must be the only twenty-four-year-old virgin left in the world!'

'It's not for lack of trying!' Vicky laughed.

As usual, when it came to discussing sexual matters, Vicky always felt as if she were Felice's younger sister, rather than the other way around. But then, in that respect she was, as Felice was far more experienced and made no attempt to pretend otherwise.

'Considering we both had the same upbringing, it's surprising we're so different,' Felice commented.

'If character only had to do with environment, the world would be full of clones!'

Felice conceded the point. 'Sometimes I wish it did, though—you're a much nicer person than me, Vicky.'

'Don't talk rubbish,' Vicky answered, embarrassed. It was rare for her sister to pay her compliments. 'As you just said, we're different—nicer doesn't come into it.'

'Okay, have it your way,' laughed Felice. 'But getting back to Barry and your particular problem, my advice is, next time you go out with him, have a few drinks to loosen yourself up. Then when he kisses you, he'll be pleasantly surprised when you ask him to make love to you properly.'

'Surprised—he'd be shocked, more likely,' Vicky smiled. 'Other than a hand on my breast under my blouse, he's behaved like a perfect gentleman.'

'Perfect idiot, you mean.' Felice closed the case she had been unpacking, which was now empty, and started on another. 'That's your trouble. All the men in your life so far have behaved like boys.'

Later, down by the swimming pool, after completing an invigorating ten lengths, Vicky thought again about what Felice had said. Without doubt there was a certain amount of truth in it. Most of the men she'd met, even at college, were unsophisticated and inexperienced, and their fumblings had irritated rather than aroused. She had longed for someone to awaken her, to excite her to a pitch where she could forget everything except the need for fulfilment.

But when it had not happened, sexual frustration, and the need to discover if she were frigid, had forced her into bed with the brother of one of Beauclare's staff, a man she had found attractive, and had also liked. But though she had enjoyed his caresses, there had been no way she could lose herself sufficiently to allow him to go all the way. He'd been furious, understandably, and even now she grew hot with embarrassment when she thought about it.

'What are you? A professional virgin?' he had demanded angrily as she'd started to dress again, after her apology had fallen on deaf ears.

'No—just a girl who can't say yes unless she's in love.'

The statement had come so naturally that she realised it was true, and it had made her wonder why it had taken her so long to perceive it. But where would she find love in Granton? It was a small town, and she not only knew most of the eligible bachelors, but at one time or another had gone out with them too. Which meant she would either have to leave Beauclare's, or hope that, once married to Barry, she would then grow to love him. Life was a series of compromises, so perhaps the sooner she accepted the fact the better. Alternatively, she could remain a virginal old maid!

Claudine herself had never shown any inclination to marry, but there was nothing old-maidish about her, or her approach to life. It was just that, until George, she had never met a man for whom she was prepared to relinquish her independence.

Vicky smiled as the object of her thoughts came in to view. Dressed, like herself, in a swimsuit—though there was rather more of it than her own minuscule bikini—Claudine came to sit beside her on a deckchair.

'Taking advantage of your last day of freedom, *chérie*?' Claudine enquired.

'The weather's so lovely, it seemed a pity not to—although there's plenty I could be doing,' Vicky added, somewhat guiltily.

'Knowing you, I'm sure that's not true. You're the most organised person I know.' Claudine squinted up at the sun. 'I hope the heatwave lasts. It will make Felice's job so much easier if our guests can spend their free time in the grounds, rather than having to organise outside activities to occupy them.'

'Where is she, by the way?'

'She borrowed my car and went into Granton. Something to do with leaving her Carmen rollers in London, and needing to do her hair this evening.'

'What on earth for? It looked perfect as it was.'

Claudine shrugged her narrow shoulders. 'You know Felice. She's never satisfied with her appearance, whatever anyone else might think.'

'Did she mention anything to you about a new boyfriend?' asked Vicky.

'Not a word.' Claudine sounded surprised. 'I assumed she was coming down here to recover from losing Chris. Truthfully, it was the main reason I agreed to give her a job when she suggested it. I thought she might be depressed, and that it would take her mind off him.'

Vicky sighed. 'If only she didn't aim so high, perhaps she wouldn't have so many disappointments.'

'Unfortunately, her head has always been turned in the wrong direction, so it's no good trying to change her.' Claudine stood up, a slight figure who looked as if a strong gust of wind could blow her away. In fact her appearance was deceptive, for she had more energy than most women half her age. 'I'm going for a swim. How about joining me?'

Felice did not materialise until dinner, joining them as they were sitting down with the rest of the staff in the dining annexe adjoining the kitchen. The meal was a high-spirited affair, helped by several bottles of wine. It would be the last completely carefree evening for some time, and it was gone midnight before the plates were stacked in the dishwasher.

'Your hair looks lovely,' Vicky remarked to Felice as they were climbing the stairs to their rooms. 'But I don't know why you bothered. You missed a perfect afternoon's sunbathing, and it will probably rain from now on!'

'Since I started doing photographic modelling I try to avoid the sun. The camera doesn't flatter a tan, and if you get strap marks it can mean losing an assignment.'

'You don't have to worry about strap marks while you're down here,' Vicky smiled. 'With no men around you can sunbathe in the nude if you like.'

'Don't be shocked, Vicky darling, but I've sunbathed in the nude *with* men around, and believe me, it's much more fun!'

'I'm not shocked, just envious,' Vicky assured her. 'Topless in St Tropez is as far as I've ever gone.'

'You'd be embarrassed there if you weren't!' Felice giggled. 'But I bet you wouldn't have even gone that far if Barry had been around.' She yawned. 'I'll feel hung-over tomorrow. Red wine always has that effect on me.'

'Me too—that's one of the reasons I prefer to stick to white.'

'With a High Court judge about to enter the family,' Felice said, 'maybe I should stick to white too. When's the wedding?'

'Lord knows. Claudine's so anxious for him not to mess up his career, she'll happily remain in the background of his life for ever.'

'More fool her,' Felice sniffed.

'That's a matter of opinion,' said Vicky. 'You've never loved a man so deeply that *his* happiness means more to you than your own. You just see them as meal tickets or sex symbols.'

Felice laughed and gave Vicky a hug, to show she didn't resent the criticism. It was one of her nicest attributes that she bore no animosity, and though it could be interpreted as a lack of sensitivity, Vicky thought it was probably better than taking things too much to heart, as she did herself.

'It's lovely having you home again,' she said quickly, 'even if it's only for a few weeks.'

'If it were for any longer, it wouldn't be so lovely!' Felice quipped. 'We're too different to live under the same roof and stay friends for long.'

Vicky smiled. Even when she was at her most exasperating, Felice's irritability was retrieved by a sense of humour, which prevented her from being completely spoiled. But then it was difficult not to spoil a girl who, having never known her own parents, had lost her adopted ones at such an early age. It had given her a sense of belonging to no one, and though Claudine had done her utmost to compensate, it had never been enough, particularly as she had found it difficult to hide her preference for Vicky. It was knowing this that made it difficult for Vicky to be as firm with her sister as she occasionally wanted.

With a sigh, Vicky climbed into bed. What had brought on this bout of analysis? Was it sour grapes because she felt discontented with her own life at the moment, and envied Felice the excitement of hers? Or was she tired and in need of a break?

Yes. That was the solution. But when she could implement it was in the lap of the gods.

CHAPTER THREE

'IF you're looking for your wife or girl-friend, I'm afraid you're in the wrong part of the house.'

Barely glancing up, Vicky addressed the man who had just pushed open the swing doors to the kitchen, where she was busily counting boxes from the Cash and Carry, the arrival of which had coincided with that of a couple of students. Leaving Claudine and Felice to welcome them, Vicky had disappeared to check off the goods.

'I'm not looking for either,' the man replied.

Vicky pushed her pencil behind her ear and gave him her full attention. He was certainly worthy of it. Tall, six-feet-two, she guessed correctly, and with a physique to match: broad-shouldered, wide-chested and with a long, loping swagger as he walked towards her, the gait heightened by his tight-fitting jeans. Beneath a blue cotton shirt his muscles rippled, and as he stopped in front of her, grey eyes regarded her with interest from a tanned face. Or maybe it wasn't a tan, she thought. Perhaps he was Italian or Greek. They often had that bronzed hue, and his hair was certainly dark enough to indicate such ancestry; black, thick and glossy, it brushed the collar of his shirt. But no, she amended. Definitely not a Latin. Apart from the height, the deep voice had been accentless.

'Then how may I help you?'

His wide mouth curved into a smile. 'By telling me who I have to see to check in.'

'Check in? I'm afraid I don't follow.'

'I'm here for the seminar,' he said. 'The name's Duncan. Jay Duncan.'

Vicky stared at him in disbelief. 'But that's not possible! J. Duncan's a woman!'

Grey eyes, almost silver in the mahogany tanned face, crinkled at the corners. 'I assure you, Miss . . .?'

'Marshall,' she informed him. 'Vicky Marshall.'

'Well, Vicky Marshall, I assure you I'm a man, and always have been. I can strip if you need further evidence.'

He looked quite capable of doing so—a man totally sure of himself, with no inhibitions.

'What I meant was, we were expecting a woman because it clearly states in our brochure we're a single sex school,' she explained.

'I haven't seen your brochure,' said Jay Duncan glibly. 'It was your reputation that brought me here.'

'I'm afraid you've had a wasted journey.' Vicky swallowed her disappointment. Goodbye cheque, hello overdraft! 'We simply don't have the facilities to accommodate both sexes.'

'I assure you I'm house-trained, and since my psychoanalysis I've given up rape!'

Vicky's lips tightened. There was no need for the heavy sarcasm. After all, she had more reason to be upset than he did.

'I mean we don't have separate bathrooms for every student, and it would mean sharing,' she elaborated. 'It might cause some embarrassment, or even resentment.'

'I don't mind using the staff bathroom, if it will help,' he suggested. 'I'm sure they'd be prepared to make the sacrifice for the kind of money I'm paying you.' His eyes moved insolently over her. 'Unless they're all frightened old maids as well?'

The implication was obvious, and Vicky felt herself reddening. In spite of his obvious attractions, he was rapidly using up her patience.

'I'll have to discuss it with Miss Beauclare before I can give you an answer,' she said stiffly, refusing to be steamrollered. 'Some women only come here because we're single sex, and there aren't any opportunities for extra-curricular activities.'

'How about if I promise to stay in my room the minute lessons are over? Or better still, stay in yours!' His cheeks dimpled winningly. 'Assuming you're not married, of course?' he added.

Little lights danced in the depths of his dark grey eyes, which were surrounded by very long, curling black lashes. There was definitely Latin blood somewhere in his genes, she decided.

'I might be prepared to share my bathroom with you,' she said coldly, 'but sharing my bed is beyond the call of duty, whatever price you're prepared to pay.'

His eyes narrowed, but the smile did not leave his face. 'My attentions are usually considered a pleasure!'

'I'm prepared to take your word for it.' She moved towards the door. 'Come with me, and I'll speak to Miss Beauclare about you now.'

Silently he walked beside her, shortening his stride to match her slower pace. She felt unusually small and fragile next to his tall, broad-shouldered frame, a sensation that made her feel somehow vulnerable as well.

Claudine was sorting out luggage in the hall, and

she looked towards Jay Duncan questioningly as they approached.

'This is *Mr* Jay Duncan,' Vicky introduced him, then without preamble went on to explain the situation.

'I think Mr Duncan's suggestion is sensible,' agreed Claudine immediately. 'But as I'm the only one with a private bathroom, it would be best if he took my room, and I'll move into the one we'd originally assigned to him.'

'That's very kind of you, Miss Beauclare, but I wouldn't dream of turning you out of your room,' protested Jay Duncan.

'It's no trouble. I'll get one of the girls to clear my things out straight away,' Claudine replied. 'But it will be at least an hour before it's ready for you to move into. Why don't you show Mr Duncan around in the meanwhile?' she addressed Vicky.

'I haven't finished checking the delivery.' Vicky grasped at the excuse.

'I'll do it,' volunteered Claudine. 'I'm sure Mr Duncan will find your company more entertaining than mine—assuming there isn't a Mrs Duncan around anywhere to object?' she added with a smile.

'Fortunately, no.'

Although irritated at Claudine's obviousness, there was little Vicky could do but comply graciously.

'How about the grounds first?' she suggested, as Claudine disappeared.

'That's fine with me.' Once again he fitted in his steps with Vicky's. 'What's your job around here?' he asked conversationally, as they reached the terrace.

'I'm deputy head and, after Miss Beauclare, the principal cookery teacher. In fact, I've volunteered for any extra tuition caused by your business commitments.'

'I hope you're not regretting it?'

She shrugged. 'As long as you stick to the rules like everyone else. We may have relaxed them by allowing you to stay, but don't expect any other preferential treatment. As far as I'm concerned, you're just another student.'

'What if I don't stick to the rules? Do I get caned?' he teased good-humouredly.

Vicky stopped at the bottom of the steps that led to the lawns, and turned to face him. 'Why have you come here, Mr Duncan? You don't strike me as the kind of man who cooks as a hobby, and wants to improve his knowledge.'

'As we've only just met, I don't see how you can judge what type of man I am,' he protested. 'But it happens, you're right. I can just about make toast without burning it.'

'In which case you should have gone to a beginner's course,' she pointed out irritably.

'But you don't do one.'

'There are plenty of schools that do. Frankly, you'll be wasting your money here.'

'Being taught by the best is never a waste of money—and I'm a fast learner.'

'What gave you the urge? Want to make someone a perfect husband?'

'I don't need cookery lessons for *that*!'

'Then why come here?' she persisted.

'I'm in the fast-food business, and I've had it in mind to open a chain of gourmet take-aways,' he said smoothly. 'I thought I'd like to find out about some of the pitfalls first.'

'Fast-food . . .' Vicky paused. Jay Duncan. Good lord, he couldn't be . . . 'Don't tell me you own Duncan Diners?'

'For my sins,' he said modestly.

'And for your customers' indigestion!'

His smile faded. 'Ever eaten in one?'

'I'd rather starve!'

'I can't bear food snobs,' he said tersely. 'Don't you know it's wrong to condemn without a trial?'

Knowing her dislike of him had made her over-vehement—though why she disliked him, she did not know—she had the grace to look ashamed.

'You're right, Mr Duncan. But, quite honestly, I'd rather have an apple and a lump of cheese than the plastic meals that pass as food in aeroplanes and your type of restaurant.' She paused. 'I still can't quite see how coming here will help you. I would have thought the pitfalls were the same whatever kind of restaurant you open.'

'I was really referring to the food. I'd like to get some ideas of the kind of dishes that are most suitable to serve.'

'You could employ a good chef to advise you.'

'There's nothing like first-hand knowledge.'

'Do you intend cooking, then?' she asked sarcastically.

'I only cook up ideas.'

I'll bet, she thought, and his leering smile told her that she had given her thoughts away. Really, he was an impossible man, as conceited as he was good-looking! And he was very good-looking.

'Any boy-friends?' he asked suddenly.

Startled, she stared up into his face. 'I beg your pardon?'

'Any boy-friends?' he repeated. 'I always like to know the competition.'

'Are you usually so blunt, Mr Duncan?' Vicky did not hide her irritation.

'I don't call it being blunt to know where I stand.'

'On the lawn of a cookery school, not the Club Méditerranée.'

'You've a nice line in wit, Vicky Marshall. But you haven't answered my question.'

'It's no concern of yours whether or not I have a boy-friend.'

'But do you?' he persisted.

'Hundreds,' she said scathingly. 'There's so much opportunity in a girls' cookery school.'

'What about when parents come to call? I bet you've had a few propositions?'

Really, the man was insufferable!

'My private life has nothing to do with you, Mr Duncan,' Vicky reiterated. 'And if you're looking for light relief in the evenings, I suggest you concentrate on the pupils rather than me.'

'I might just do that,' he said agreeably. 'It mightn't do much for your school's reputation, though.'

The desire to hit him was so strong that Vicky's palms tingled. She could envisage all sorts of problems with this arrogant male and, had they not needed the money desperately, she would have suggested to Claudine that she give him back his cheque and send him packing.

'You can't do that,' the man said, once again guessing her thoughts. 'You've already accepted my money, and that means we have a contract.'

'Nevertheless it implies proper behaviour on the part of both parties,' Vicky retorted. 'And you'd do well to remember that, Mr Duncan.'

'Are you always on the defensive with men?'

'Oh, there you are, Vicky darling.'

Felice bore down on them, obviating Vicky's reply.
The girl looked delectably cool in a kanga lawn dress,
its misty greens accentuating her beautiful Titian hair.

'Are you one of our fathers?' she twinkled up at Jay.

'I started young,' he said solemnly, 'but not as young
as all that.'

'Mr Duncan's one of our pupils,' Vicky said coldly.

'Wow!' said Felice, still looking at him. 'What can
we teach *you*?'

Vicky wished she could give her sister a surrepti-
tious kick, but she knew it would do no good. In the
circle she moved in, this kind of sexual repartee was
second nature, but if Claudine heard it, she'd have no
compunction in cutting Felice down to size.

'Are you one of the pupils?' Jay Duncan was saying.

'I'm Vicky's sister,' Felice replied. 'But I'm helping
out here for a short time between engagements.'

'Of the matrimonial kind?'

She laughed. 'Modelling and TV commercials.'

As her sister spoke, Vicky couldn't help wondering
whether Felice had found out that Jay Duncan was
intending to come down here. Her sister had many
contacts, and she'd put nothing past her. Not that she
blamed her for trying to get a job from this man. After
all, he spent a fortune on advertising, and once you
became a Duncan Dolly Bird, your face was plastered
over hoardings and television screens for months. It
was exactly the boost Felice needed to set her career
alight. Yet if she got personally involved with a man
like this, she might well get her fingers burned. Not for
the first time she wished her impressionable younger

sister had taken up a more mundane career that would not have laid her open to the temptations that this one did.

'Don't just stand there, darling,' Felice said, giving her a little push. 'There's absolute chaos in the kitchen, with groceries stacked all over the place, and no one knowing where to put them.'

'Claudine said she'd see to it.'

'She must have forgotten.'

Vicky knew her sister was lying, yet was in no mood to quarrel with her.

'Then perhaps you'll show Mr Duncan around while I sort things out?'

'May I help you?' the man beside her said. 'With me beside you, you won't need a ladder to reach the top cupboards.'

'I won't need a ladder anyway,' Vicky said sweetly. 'We always put the provisions within easy reach. That's something you'd have learned if you'd taken a beginner's course somewhere else.'

'Perhaps you can give me extra tuition.'

'You'll already be getting extra tuition,' she said coldly.

'I'm willing to have more—and pay for it too.'

'Do you think money can buy you everything?'

'Almost,' he said. 'Don't you?'

'No, I don't.' Not giving him a chance to reply, Vicky swung away from him.

Changing for dinner—which Claudine always insisted they did—Vicky resisted putting on one of her prettier dresses, afraid that Jay Duncan would think she was dressing up for him. Drat the man! He'd been popping into her thoughts ever since she'd met him, and since she didn't even like him, it only went to show how much she needed the company of a sexually forceful male. She sighed. If only Barry were less nice, and more demanding. But the trouble was, he took no for an answer without ever asking the question! Buttoning up her shirt-waister, and tugging a comb through her hair, she went downstairs.

There were twelve pupils only, the usual mix of young, upper-class housewives, middle-aged ladies happy to while away their time by learning how to improve their cooking, and a couple of home economics students, anxious to give a touch of class to their City and Guilds course.

Jay Duncan, the only male, stood out like a sore thumb. But it was a thumb everyone wanted to attatch themselves to, and all the women were hovering around him, even Claudine, who was dispensing sherry, and smiling at something he had said. With surprise Vicky noticed a magnum of champagne cooling in an ice-bucket, and her soft mouth tightened. So he was trying to ingratiate himself, was he?

'You're just in time for the champagne,' he said, aware of her entry even though he'd had his back to the door.

'I don't like champagne,' she lied. 'It makes me burp.'

'Musically, I bet.'

She was hard put not to laugh, but had no intention of letting him see it.

'If you really don't like the bubbles,' he went on, 'I'll buy you a swizzle stick.'

'Gold, of course,' she quipped, and was surprised to see a momentary hardening in his eyes.

'Naturally,' he said. 'Beautiful girls have a right to expect the best, and you're exceptionally beautiful.'

'Don't overdo the flattery, Mr Duncan,' she said sharply. 'I've no false modesty, and I know I'm pretty, but no more than that.'

She went to move past him, but he blocked her way, his head slightly to one side as he eyed her. She had the impression he was studying her carefully, not in the light-hearted manner she would have expected, but with an intentness that bespoke something else, something she couldn't define.

'Classy,' he murmured. 'That's what you are. Beautiful and classy. You're the one who should be a model, not your sister.'

'Felice is gorgeous!' Vicky expostulated.

'So are thousands of other girls. But it's having a touch of class that sets a girl apart, and you've got it, Vicky Marshall.'

'Are you asking me to be a Duncan Dolly Bird, then?'

'No, Jay Duncan's girl,' he said quietly. 'How about it?'

'Don't you ever take no for an answer? I've no desire to be one of the flock.'

'Would you be interested in being the only one?'

Vicky stared into his eyes. This was too ridiculous. She'd only met this man a few hours ago and here he was propositioning her with all seriousness. Or was he? She was out of her depth with a man of this type, and didn't know quite what to say or how to act. All she knew was that she couldn't go on being rude to him, or it would disrupt the mood of the class and affect everyone. But nor could she take him seriously.

'I wish you wouldn't talk to me like this, Mr Duncan,' she said quietly. 'We don't run this school for love but for money, and it's very important to us that this course is a success. If you're going to persist in flirting with me——'

'What makes you think I'm flirting?'

'It can't be anything else. You barely know me.'

'Don't you believe in love at first sight?'

'No, I don't——'

'I think the champagne's cold enough now.'

This was from Claudine, and Jay Duncan went swiftly over to the ice-bucket and opened the champagne. As the cork popped and the liquid frothed into goblets, Vicky moved to a corner of the room and watched everyone. Jay Duncan was the centre of all eyes again, and loving it, and Vicky chided herself for having been silly enough for thinking he might have been serious a moment ago. It was obviously second nature to the man to come on with every female. Look at the deferential way he was pouring champagne for Mrs Smythe-Browne. Sixty if a day, and sixteen stone with it! Yet it was nice of him too, for the woman had been recently widowed and had come on this course in the hope of getting out of her depression.

'Quite an eyeful, isn't he?' Claudine was standing beside her. 'I've a feeling this seminar is going to be different from all the others.'

'You can say that again,' said Vicky sourly.

'Don't you like him?' The woman looked surprised.

'I don't think I do. There's something odd about him.'

'You're the one who's odd, my dear. You're too much on the defensive with men. You should be more like Felice.'

'How much more like?' Vicky asked, faintly irritated.

'Well, not *that* much,' Claudine conceded with a chuckle. 'But enough like her to enjoy a good-looking man like Mr Duncan without thinking in terms of commitment and for ever.'

'You're a fine one to talk,' Vicky said softly. 'Look at the way you're holding back with George, when the poor man is simply dying to——'

'He's already married,' Claudine said swiftly, 'and I don't want to do anything that would jeopardise his career.'

'Maybe he's decided that personal happiness is more important. Anyway, in this day and age I don't think his career would be affected by a divorce, particularly when his wife is such a——'

'Hush,' Claudine said, putting a restraining hand on Vicky's arm. 'I don't want to talk about it any more. Just remember, *ma chère*, that you can't compare my life with yours. You're young, and you should live a little. Throw your hat over the windmill before you settle down.'

'I tried that once,' Vicky reminded her, 'but when it came to it I couldn't say yes.'

'Then try again—you know the old saying—if at first you don't succeed . . .'

Claudine's advice, coming so soon after her talk with Felice, kept popping into Vicky's mind throughout the evening, although, watching her sister throw herself at Jay Duncan, she couldn't see herself having even a transitory affair with him. He was certainly entering into the spirit of things, and although intuition told her the sort of life he lived, he was behaving this evening with perfect propriety.

Dinner at night was served in Claudine's private dining-room, since the number of pupils was small.

Normally part of the meal had been prepared earlier in the day by the pupils themselves, with one elaborate dish generally done by the resident chef, who also prepared weekend meals and breakfast. Serving was done by two women who came in from the nearby village, the permanent staff being away for the school vacation.

Jay Duncan took it on himself to serve the wines, and though he said loudly that he knew nothing whatever about cooking, he admitted to knowing something about the grape. Indeed, he proved himself highly knowledgeable, and he and Claudine had a long discourse on the merits of Californian red as compared with French.

'Will you be serving wine with your gourmet take-away food?' Felice asked, anxious to bring his attention back to herself.

'I hadn't thought of it,' he said, 'but it's not a bad idea.'

'Will you be opening new places, or changing some of your present ones?'

'I'm not touching Duncan Diners,' he said positively. 'You don't kill the goose when it's laying golden eggs.'

'What are you going to call the new chain?' one of the other women asked.

'The name's still under wraps,' he smiled.

Watching the ease with which he parried the questions levied at him, Vicky realised that he was a far more intelligent man than she had first given him credit for. His easy assurance and swift repartee had made her suppose him to be the average tycoon, high in bankable assets but not necessarily in mental ones. But Jay Duncan was different. He had a sharp mind behind the banter, and it would be as well to remember that. She frowned. Somehow it didn't ring true that he was here to learn about cooking. Yet the reasons he'd given were valid, and since she couldn't think of any other motive why he should be here, she had no choice but to accept him at face value.

CHAPTER FOUR

JAY DUNCAN lay back on the bed in his room smoking a cigar. So far, things had gone better than expected. True, for a few moments he'd had something of a fright when Vicky had realised he was here as a pupil and had said it was impossible for him to stay, but thanks to some quick wit, everything had turned out all right. And it was imperative to his future that it continued to do so.

His mind went back to that fateful day two weeks ago, the day that had made it necessary for him to attend this cookery course at any cost.

He'd been signing a batch of letters when his intercom had buzzed.

'Mrs Lydia Walton to see you,' his secretary had informed him.

Now what could *she* want? he had thought irritably. Surely she wasn't collecting for another of her charities? He'd given her two large cheques already this month, and on the last occasion she'd wasted over an hour of his time afterwards with trivial chatter. Well, he wouldn't give her the opportunity of doing the same thing again. He had a busy day ahead of him: lunch at Scott's with his broker, then back to his office to finalise ideas with the agency responsible for the advertising campaign being launched in the winter for his fast-food chain, Duncan Diners. Finding the right girl for the commercials was all-important, and might also be fun, and he'd arranged to sit in on the tests.

'Ask her to come in—and interrupt us in ten minutes with an urgent phone call from the States,' he instructed, *sotto voce*.

A few moments later the door opened and a woman entered. Slim, honey-blonde, and elegantly dressed, she had a quiet beauty that came from the perfect symmetry of her features. She had been a top fashion model in her youth, and though she was now in her early forties, her looks had hardly diminished. If they needed more time and care to sustain them, it was barely discernible, for the only make-up visible was the rose colour on her mouth, and the soft brown shadow on the eyelids.

'I hope I'm not taking you away from anything important,' she said apologetically, closing the door and coming further into the room.

'You are.' Jay's smile as he stood to greet her robbed the words of terseness. 'But welcome all the same.'

'I wouldn't have bothered you if it hadn't been absolutely necessary.' She sank gracefully on to a cream leather armchair next to his desk.

'Who do I make the cheque out to?' Jay asked, reaching for the drawer containing his cheque book.

Lydia Walton gave him a puzzled look. 'I don't understand.'

'Which of your charities is in urgent need of funds this time?' Jay's dark brows, thick and well curved, met above his long, straight nose as he smiled, and seated himself again.

'I'm not here collecting money.' She hesitated. 'It's something far more important and personal.'

'What, exactly?' he prompted.

Limpid blue eyes widened. 'It's George,' she said, naming her husband. 'He's . . . he's having an affair.'

Jay had made no effort to hide his surprise. Not because he imagined Lydia and her husband to be idyllically happy—at best their relationship could be described as polite—but because she had chosen to confide in him. Although he was extremely fond of George—his father's best friend, whom he regarded almost as an uncle—his feelings for Lydia verged on dislike, and he knew she was well aware of it. There was something about her that repelled him—a kind of smugness, a contentment that came less from inner security than from conceit. Certainly he was an unlikely candidate for her marital problems.

'How serious is it?' Jay asked aloud.

'He's supposed to be thinking things over, but I can tell he's already made up his mind to leave me. He's convinced this is the love of his life, and that his money and position have nothing whatever to do with it.'

'Who is she? Anyone you know?'

'She works at Beauclare's, and taught Caroline when she was there.' Lydia named the famous residential cookery school where her daughter had been a pupil. 'George always visited far more frequently than I—though at the time I put it down to over-filial devotion. Now I realise it was because of this girl.' She leaned forward, and the musky perfume that he always associated with her wafted into his nostrils. 'I've invested too much of my life in George to lose him now to a twenty-four-year-old nobody, just because she's good in bed and makes him feel young again.'

Lydia's outburst was so contrary to her normal calm and controlled manner that it gave a clear indication of the strain she was under, and had Jay not perceived

that her motives were entirely selfish, he might even
have felt sorry for her. But her concern had nothing to
do with keeping home and family together, or with
George's career—rather, it was with *her* career, as
George's wife, and the reflected glory of her position.

He tried to visualise George, level-headed, staid,
and fifty-eight, sacrificing his all—which was very
considerable—for a girl more than thirty years his
junior. It was almost too ludicrous to contemplate. He
was an extremely eminent Queen's Counsel, and there
were rumours of a title in the next Birthday Honours.

'I'm sorry, of course,' Jay told her truthfully. 'But I
fail to see how I can help. Marriage counselling is
hardly my line.'

'I agree—that's why I thought action would be more
appropriate than words.'

Jay raised an eyebrow enquiringly. 'What kind of
action were you thinking of?'

'That you meet her, and get her to fall in love with
you.'

For an instant Jay thought he had not heard
correctly. But one look at Lydia's determined expression confirmed that he had.

'Are you serious?'

'I've never been more serious about anything in my
life.' Lydia's voice was hard. 'It's obvious this girl is
only interested in George because of his money and
position—why else would she want to marry a man of
his age?'

'She could be in love with him—it has been known
to happen,' Jay interjected drily.

'Perhaps with glamorous figures like film stars or
tycoons, but George hardly comes into that category.

He may be sensational addressing a jury, but out of court he's an absolute bore!'

'Far less of one than most of the film stars and tycoons *I've* met,' asserted Jay honestly. 'Perhaps you find him boring because you've never been interested in what he has to say.'

She shrugged. 'Okay, so I'm no intellectual. But you can't tell me his interest in this girl is a meeting of the minds. For God's sake, she teaches cookery!'

'Don't they say the way to a man's heart is through his stomach?'

'George doesn't know the difference between a mar*mite* and Marmite, so I doubt they talk recipes!' Lydia paused, and ran the tip of her tongue over her lower lip. 'I'm sure you'll have no difficulty with her. You're young, intelligent, good-looking and rich. George won't stand a chance by comparison.'

'It sounds as if you're reciting one of my publicity blurbs!' Jay joked. 'But I'm afraid flattery will get you nowhere.'

'Why? Don't you think my idea is a good one?'

'Yes—if she's as calculating as you assume.'

'Then what's the problem?'

'I don't think I've any right to interfere. This is something that only concerns you and George.' Jay picked up a pencil and twirled it between his hands; he had large hands but beautifully shaped, with well cared-for nails and strong thumbs. 'My advice is for you to play the waiting game. He's not a fool, and if the girl really is a gold-digger, then I'm sure he'll eventually come to his senses and realise it.'

'By then it could be too late, and his career could be in ruins.'

'I think you're exaggerating the situation. Extra-marital affairs are hardly a cause for comment, even with public figures like George. It may delay his appointment for a while, but once things return to normal . . .' Jay shrugged. 'I'm fond of you both, and naturally I'll be sorry if things don't work out, but I'm sure——'

'Do stop pretending, Jay! Hypocrisy isn't your style,' Lydia interrupted impatiently. 'You don't like me, and you won't give a damn if George leaves me. But I've no intention of allowing some little country bumpkin to become Lady Walton before I do—even if I have to resort to blackmail to stop it.'

'Blackmail?' said Jay with an indulgent smile. 'Now what guilty dark secret would George have to hide?'

'I wasn't thinking of George,' replied Lydia with a meaningful glance.

Jay smiled again. 'I can't imagine that you've discovered anything about *me* that hasn't already appeared in *Private Eye*.'

'You're an excellent liar, Jay. If I didn't know better, you'd have me convinced,' she answered smoothly.

With an effort Jay controlled his anger, though the urge to be rude was becoming overwhelming.

But his voice was, as before, mild. 'It seems you know me better than I know myself. Perhaps you'll enlighten me.'

Lydia lowered her head and hunched her shoulders forward. 'I know you're Mark Mason.' She held up a rose-tipped hand as he started to speak. 'Don't bother to deny it, because I have a letter signed by you that proves it.'

Shocked out of his complacency, Jay stared at her. 'How did you find out?'

'One weekend George brought a file home with your name on it, and I became curious when he refused to discuss what was in it. As soon as he retired for his afternoon nap, I peeped at it. It appeared you were having trouble with your first publisher over royalties, and wanted to get out of your contract.'

'And you stole the letter then, I presume?'

'Borrowed,' she corrected with a smile. 'And when you've done as I've asked, you can have it back.'

'Do you always go through your husband's private files?' he questioned coldly.

'Yes—whenever I think they might be of interest to me.' Lydia's voice was clear as a bell as she defied the implied criticism.

'Why haven't you said anything about it before?'

'There wasn't any need, and if you'd agreed to do as I asked without arguing, I wouldn't have mentioned it now, either. I know I sound a bitch, but that's only because you've forced the issue.'

'And if I refuse?'

'I'll give the story to the newspapers, and Mark Mason, alias Jay Duncan, high priest of fast-food, will become a laughing stock.'

Jay swore silently. If Lydia wasn't a bitch, she was giving a very good imitation of one!

'It looks as if I have no choice,' he said aloud.

Lydia lowered her eyelids to hide her triumph, but she could not keep victory from her voice.

'You're a man after my own heart,' she said silkily. 'You know when you're beaten, and don't waste time prevaricating.'

He shrugged his powerful shoulders. 'As you hold all the cards, there wouldn't be much point.' His intercom buzzed, and he flicked the switch connecting him to his secretary. 'Yes?'

'A phone call from New York,' she announced. 'Shall I put it through?'

'No—tell them I'll phone back in five minutes,' he instructed.

'It's extremely urgent,' she persisted.

'So is the matter I'm dealing with at the moment,' he answered tersely. He would have to apologise to Madge later for his contradictory behaviour.

'I've a photograph of the girl,' Lydia said, as he turned his attention back to her. 'I found it in George's pocket and had a copy made,' she explained, holding it out to him. 'Poor poppet; he searched frantically for it before finding it a couple of days later under the driving seat of his car.'

Jay glanced at it. There were two women in the head-and-shoulder picture; one, young and pretty, the other, sharp-featured and in her mid-fifties, with no attempt made to disguise it. She was not unattractive though, in spite of lines and greying hair. Was she the younger girl's mother, perhaps? Certainly she bore no resemblance, but then there was nothing unusual in that. He concentrated again on George's friend. Serious-eyed, clear complexion, thick black hair, nice nose and mouth, good bones. Good figure too, if the nicely rounded shoulders were anything to go by. He was pleasantly surprised at George's taste. Somehow he'd imagined a vacuous well-stacked blonde—wasn't that the type most middle-aged men preferred?—but this girl looked like class, in every sense of the word.

'Victoria Marshall's her name.' Lydia's voice cut into his thoughts. 'She's deputy headmistress, and Caroline admired her enormously. Obviously she's no fool, and realised the best way to George's heart was through his daughter.'

'Where *is* Caroline, by the way?' asked Jay.

'In the States, cooking for a friend who's just had twins. Now to get back to this Marshall girl ...'

'How am I supposed to meet this *femme fatale?*' enquired Jay sourly. 'The school's in the country, so I'm hardly likely to bump into her.'

'I'm sure love will find a way,' said Lydia carelessly. 'I'll leave you with a brochure of the school—it might give you some ideas.'

She reached into her handbag and took out a glossy folder, with a picture of an attractive Georgian manor house on the front.

'In other words, you've left me to do all the homework?'

'Don't sound so grumpy, Jay. Thank your lucky stars she isn't fat and forty. At least an affair with her won't be too much of a hardship.'

'I'm more concerned with George's reaction when he finds out. He probably won't thank me for interfering.'

'Don't lose any sleep over it. Once you've shown her up for what she really is, he'll bless you for saving him from making a fool of himself.' Lydia rose, and moved to the door. 'You'll have the field clear until the beginning of September. George is leaving next month for a judicial tour of Australia.'

'You're not going with him?'

'I prefer the South of France, so I'm going down to the villa.'

'Have a nice time,' he said, for the benefit of his secretary who could see and hear them through the open door. The way he felt about Lydia at the moment, he could cheerfully have strangled her.

'I will,' she smiled, 'especially now I know you're looking after my interests!'

Sourly Jay returned to his desk and placed the brochure of Beauclare's in front of him. But he did not examine it immediately. Instead his thoughts turned to what Lydia had asked him to do. He had no choice but to agree, and while his motives were not altruistic, he might indeed be doing George a favour by showing the girl up for what she was. Anyway, when you boiled it all down, this whole predicament was George's fault in the first place. If he hadn't brought that damn file home and left it lying around, Lydia would never have discovered his secret—a secret that Jay had kept from the public since he'd submitted his first article as a food critic for the rag week edition of his university's magazine.

It had been about an Oxford restaurant, and he'd used a pseudonym because he was dating the owner's daughter. The article had been highly critical, though amusing, and had attracted the notice of a local newspaper. The editor had asked him to do a monthly column in the same light-hearted vein, and this had led to it being syndicated in a national daily.

Within a year he had become a household name, and this had led him to writing food guides, bought as much for their witticisms as his criticisms. Recently he had produced another bestseller; a compilation of recipes of the famous, complete with details of their careers and backgrounds, and lavish coloured pictures of them, taken in their dining-rooms and kitchens by one of the most prestigious photographers of the day.

As a gimmick, he had continued to use his *nom de plume*, keeping his identity a secret from all except his family, and those to whom the knowledge was essential. The mystery surrounding him created endless speculation in the media, who would have paid a fortune to discover the identity of 'Mark Mason'.

But his cover was perfect. At twenty-five he had returned from a year studying the American fast-food business, to turn his staid, family-owned chain of small cafés into a fast-growing rival to McDonald's.

In public he made his dislike of gourmet cooking well known, although in private he was knowledgeable and discerning on the subject. But as head of Duncan Diners he sneered at the élitism of the 'starred' restaurants, and proudly boasted that his own chain could compete with them any day—as long as you weren't looking for fancy sauces which often disguised poor ingredients, and elaborate presentation which resulted in fancy prices.

The quintessential English flavour of the food he offered had been as much responsible for its success as anything else, particularly in the States, but Jay's claim that cheap did not necessarily mean nasty was no idle boast. Duncan Diners, though uniform in size and design, were spotlessly clean, and pleasing to the eye. Service was hurried but always polite, and quantity was never used as a substitute for quality. This made them slightly up-market, but earned customer satisfaction, and ensured the lowest complaint rate of any fast-food chain in the world.

Jay yawned and stubbed out his cigar, his mind returning to the present. He had every right to be proud of his success. At thirty-three, his 'Mark Mason' books alone had made him a millionaire—no mean achievement when one considered the intense competition. But now he had to accede to Lydia's demands or his secret would finally be revealed, which meant he had to give that spiky little schoolmarm, Victoria Marshall, a lesson in love she would never forget.

CHAPTER FIVE

THE first complete day of the course was normally devoted to cookery, though subsequent days were also given over to the many leisure activities that were so much part of this seminar, and which also made it unique.

'You are here,' Claudine told her students that first morning, 'in order to improve your culinary ability, and to help you become the hostess with the mostest!'

Everyone brightened at the thought of this, and made sure all their cooking utensils were set out properly in front of them, and their notebooks and pens were at the ready.

The class was held in one of the demonstration kitchens. There were six tables, with two pupils sharing each. Pink gingham aprons were provided by the school, with capacious front pockets. Matching headbands were also provided, and Claudine was insistent that they all wore them, saying that there was nothing worse than finding hair in one's food.

'We won't be doing very elaborate dishes the first day,' the principal said. 'Cheese soufflé with a prawn sauce, individual Beef Wellingtons, and Tarte Tatin. Vicky and I are your instructors, and Clarissa and Jane, whom we call our terrible twins,' there was general laughter at this, 'will help you with the clearing up. After all, this is a holiday and we don't want you going home with dishpan hands! Now then, ladies, all the ingredients for the meal have been weighed out and will be found on the shelf underneath your table. Should you need additional provisions, ask Vicky or myself. The recipes are set out on the leaflets in front of you, but Vicky and I will be walking around watching you, and when there's anything complicated to be done, we will be giving you a demonstration first.'

'What do you call complicated?' a male voice asked from the doorway, and all eyes swivelled to see Jay Duncan.

Everybody burst out laughing, and even Vicky permitted herself a smile at the sight of the broad-shouldered frame in a pink gingham apron that barely covered his chest and stopped well above the knees of his jeans. He had tied his headband around his forehead and a quiff of dark hair fell over it. As a means of keeping his hair off his face it was hopeless, but it gave him the swaggering air of a pirate that was infinitely attractive.

'You're late, Mr Duncan,' Claudine said.

'Blame that on your magnificent swimming pool,' he said unashamedly. 'I've just done a hundred lengths.'

'I hope you won't be too tired to do any cooking,' Vicky said sweetly.

'Just watch me,' he replied, and loped over to the table he had been assigned with Mrs Smythe-Browne, all of whose chins quivered happily as he did so.

It took a moment before everyone settled down again, and Vicky vowed to have a word with Jay Duncan. It was hard enough teaching twelve pupils at the best of times, without having him causing any lack of concentration.

Soon everyone in the class was busy whipping up the egg whites for the soufflés. These were competent cooks, after all, and the whole of the day's menu was

easy. Except to Jay Duncan. He was all fingers and
thumbs. Toes too, Vicky thought, looking at the egg
whites spattered on his shoes. What a colossal nerve
he had, coming on a course like this. Not that the other
women seemed to mind. They practically fell over
themselves offering to help him, coming to his aid
before Claudine or Vicky could. And how happily he
accepted it, like a potentate with his harem! Sitting
astride his stool, arms akimbo as they peeled the
prawns for him and made the sauce, beat the yolks and
folded them into the whites, and even placed the
finished dish in the oven, in case he burned his fingers.
It was just as bad with the next course, which Mrs
Smythe-Browne insisted on doing for him, only
allowing him to weigh the flour and butter for the
pastry, and to carry the dishes over to the sink for
Clarissa and Jane to wash.

'I think we should allow our budding chef to do the
Tarte Tatin by himself,' Vicky said at noon. 'After all,
he is here to learn how to cook, and he won't always
have you lovely ladies to help him.'

Grinning broadly, he set about peeling the apples,
and Vicky watched in horror as most of the apple went
off with the rind, leaving little more than a core to be
put into the pie dish.

'I'm afraid I'll need some more apples,' he said in a
tone of dismay.

'You wouldn't if you knew how to peel them
properly,' Vicky retorted and, taking the knife from
his fingers, deftly showed him, unable to resist peeling
a large Bramley without breaking the skin.

'Brilliant!' he said, admiring the almost translucent,
long circular strip of rind. 'What do I do with the apple
now?'

'Read the recipe, Mr Duncan,' Vicky snapped, and

watched as he began to cut the apples into hunks.

'We *slice* the apples, Mr Duncan!' she grabbed his hand to stop him chopping up another one. 'The whole purpose is to arrange them in elegant slices. Haven't you ever had Tarte Tatin?'

He shook his head. 'If we don't serve it at Duncan Diners, I don't know it.'

'You mean you only eat your own fast-food?'

'Sure. You must come out for dinner with me one night and try them. You don't know what you're missing.'

'I prefer ignorance.'

'Mr Duncan's chain is better than anyone else's,' one of the younger women said, casting him sheep's eyes. 'My children insist on going there whenever we go out for a meal.'

'How old are they?' Vicky asked.

'Eight and ten.'

Vicky's eyes spoke volumes, and the woman had the grace to blush. 'Well, those sort of eating places do serve a need to the public,' she defended herself, 'and one can't eat gourmet food all the time.'

'I agree,' said Jay Duncan, tipping half a bag of flour into a pastry bowl and chucking in a lump of butter.

'Weigh the ingredients,' Vicky bit out at him.

He gave her a look of innocence. 'I thought good cooks went by instinct.'

'*Good* cooks do, Mr Duncan. That's why *you* should weigh everything.'

'I've a feeling you're getting at me,' he said.

'I hadn't realised you were so sensitive.'

He opened his mouth to reply, then thought better of it, and obediently yanked out the lump of butter and then tipped the flour on to the scales.

It was a similar story when it came to rolling out the pastry.

'We use the centre of the rolling pin, Mr Duncan. The knobs at the end are for holding, not banging out the dough.'

'My, you live and learn, don't you?'

'*Most* people do, but with you I think it's going to be an uphill struggle!'

'I'll have you eating those words,' he warned.

'So far that's infinitely preferable to eating your cooking!'

But at the end of the day, the meal he'd prepared, or rather had helped to prepare, while it did not compare to the other students' efforts, was quite palatable.

'How about some of my upside-down apple pie?' He proffered his plate towards Vicky.

'You mean Tarte Tatin, don't you?' she asked frostily, guessing he was being deliberately obtuse.

He shrugged. 'Why give it a fancy French name when our common language is English? I find that sort of thing infuriating in restaurants as well. It's pure pretension.'

'I think that's an over-reaction. It's tradition, that's all.'

'Whatever you want to call it. It can sometimes be embarrassing for those who don't understand French. Thank heavens a few places are beginning to realise it, and offer an English translation as well.'

'It's the language of great chefs because it's so lyrical. Let's face it, Pieds de Porc Grillé sounds a hell of a lot more appetising than Broiled Pigs' Feet, as does Cervelles au Beurre Noir Noisette than Brains in Brown Butter.'

Jay chuckled. 'You have a point there, Miss Marshall.'

After dinner, a couple of the women retired to their rooms, exhausted after the day's lessons, but Mrs Smythe-Browne and three others settled down to a game of bridge, while the remainder either read, or sat in front of the television in Claudine's private sitting-room.

'How about a stroll in the garden?' Jay Duncan suggested to Vicky as she was about to go upstairs. 'It's a beautiful night.'

'Sorry, I'm going out.'

'Alone?'

'No.'

'Would three be a crowd?' he asked.

'Yes.'

'In other words your companion is a man?'

'If we're playing Twenty Questions, then the answer is, you're getting warm!' she said sarcastically.

'You're the most exasperating female I've ever met! Why are you always on the defensive with me? I'm not going to eat you.' His eyes moved warmly over her. 'Not that you don't look good enough to eat,' he added with a wide grin. 'I'd rather have you than Beef Wellington any day!'

'As a lover of good food, I'm afraid I can't return the compliment.'

His eyes narrowed and he moved away from her, putting his hands into the pockets of his trousers. They were cut so tight that she was surprised he had any room to do so, and purposefully she avoided looking at the clearly defined curves of his hips and the sinewy muscles of his thighs.

'When I'm not acting like a city-slicker, I'm quite a nice guy, you know.'

It was an old-fashioned expression, and quite out of character, and Vicky glanced at him with surprise.

'I'm well aware of the impression I give,' he said, his voice unexpectedly serious.

'Doesn't it bother you?'

'Why should it? It's what I think of other people that counts! That's one of the advantages of having money. You can be independent of everyone's opinions.'

'Then why are you apologising for yourself now?'

'Because you're an exception to the rule,' he said softly. 'I do care what *you* think of me.'

In spite of herself she was flattered, though she refused to let him see it.

'You're wasting your time on me, Mr Duncan. I have a steady boy-friend and I'm very fond of him.'

'That's not what I heard from Felice.'

'She shouldn't have discussed my private life with you—and you'd no right to ask her,' Vicky said angrily.

'If you'd been more co-operative it wouldn't have been necessary.'

Before she could answer, the lounge door opened and Felice appeared.

'I wondered what had happened to you.' Her voice was deliberately casual. 'You said you were going to get some ice for your drink and I thought you must be waiting for it to freeze.'

'Well, I have been at the end of a cold blast, but I think I'll survive.'

'To fight another day?' Vicky said. 'I don't advise it.'

'We may give advice, but we can never prompt behaviour,' he quoted.

'I wish I knew what you two were talking about,' complained Felice, looking from one to the other.

'Nothing of any importance,' Vicky assured her,

adding, 'I'll say goodnight. I'm off to the films with Barry.'

'Funny, that's just what I felt like doing,' the man said, 'only I wasn't aware there was a cinema nearby.'

'There isn't—or at least not what *you'd* call a cinema,' Vicky said discouragingly. 'Most of the springs have gone from the seats, and the acoustics aren't great either. You have to be a real devotee to go there.'

'I am,' he assured her, nonplussed. 'How about coming with me, Felice?'

'I'd love to,' the girl said immediately. 'What's showing, Vicky?'

'*The Philadelphia Story*, with Cary Grant and Katharine Hepburn. It's as old as the hills, and it's been on television dozens of times.'

'One of my favourites,' claimed Jay Duncan, not giving Felice time to reply. 'It never palls, and part of the fun is knowing what comes next.' He smiled. 'Why don't we join up with you? Or would Barry object?'

At that moment the front doorbell chimed.

'That's probably him now, so you can ask him yourself,' said Felice, moving forward to answer it.

If Barry was irritated by the request, he was too well mannered to show it, but Vicky sensed his dislike of the other man immediately.

'We may as well all go in one car,' Jay Duncan suggested.

'Unlike London, there's no difficulty with parking,' Vicky said pointedly.

'Oh—are you two going on somewhere afterwards, then?' Jay asked with deliberate innocence. 'We don't want to spoil your plans, do we, Felice?'

Felice giggled. 'There's nowhere *to* go afterwards. Granton isn't exactly Sin City!'

'We usually have a drink at the Pig and Whistle,' explained Barry stiffly. 'But of course you're welcome to join us.'

The women disappeared to fetch their cardigans, leaving the two men making small talk in the hall. But by the time they returned, Vicky noticed that Barry's lips were tightly set. What on earth had Jay Duncan been saying to him? she wondered. Drat the man. He seemed intent on creating mischief. Why else had he lied about wanting to go to the cinema, and then refused to heed her discouraging hints. Hints? She couldn't have made it plainer that he was unwelcome unless she'd spelt it out.

'Nice car,' Jay remarked, as they climbed into Barry's Volvo. 'How many miles to the gallon does she do?'

Barry cheered slightly at this enquiry. He liked nothing better than talking cars, and if the conversation that followed was any indication, he had found a soul-mate in Jay Duncan.

The cinema was almost empty—it was an unusually warm night, and the season of Golden Movie Greats was not proving particularly popular. But Jay had not pretended when he'd said *The Philadelphia Story* was one of his favourite movies, and Vicky, who spent more time glancing in his direction than at the screen, saw him watching it intently.

'However good *High Society* was, it's not a patch on the original,' he opined, his arm linked companionably in Felice's as they strolled towards the Pig and Whistle, which was only a couple of blocks away from the cinema. 'Grant and Hepburn are incomparable.'

'As you're such an old movie buff, you won't be bored down here, Mr Duncan,' Vicky couldn't stop herself from saying. 'The season doesn't finish for another couple of weeks, and there's a different film on every night.'

'You sound as if you'd like to be rid of me, Miss Marshall,' he grinned.

'For heaven's sake, why don't you call her Vicky?' said Felice. 'All this Miss Marshall, Mr Duncan stuff is a bit out of date, isn't it?'

'I think Vicky is doing it to keep me in my place,' Jay Duncan replied, losing no time in taking up Felice's invitation. 'I'm not her favourite pupil.'

'I'll try not to make it so obvious.' Vicky's tone dripped honey. 'It would never do for you to get a persecution complex.'

'Don't worry—I won't write home to Mummy and Daddy asking them to take me away!' he mocked good-humouredly.

'Did you go to boarding-school as a child?' asked Felice curiously.

'Yes—and hated it,' he answered seriously. 'I'll never put *my* kids through that particular hell.'

'Strange,' Barry said. 'I loved every minute of it. But then I was good at games, and I'm inclined to think the athletic chaps have the best of it.'

'How right you are, and what an indictment on our educational system!' Jay said forcefully. 'After I'd had my arm broken twice at rugger I refused to play for my school again, and was given a hard time of it by most of the staff and boys until one day I left. No bad thing, mind you. It prepared me for future knocks in everyday life.'

'It's not much different for girls,' Vicky said. 'I remember at our school, everyone had a crush on the games captain and dreamed of taking her place.'

'Except me,' Felice asserted. 'Muscles are all right

on men, but they don't do much for a girl unless she wants to be an all-in wrestler!'

'I don't think Vicky looks too bad on it,' Barry interjected. 'And she's good at most sports.'

By now they had reached the pub, and with Barry to the forefront they pushed their way through the crowd to the bar.

'Now we know why the cinema was empty,' remarked Jay. 'It looks as if the whole town's congregated in here.'

'There are four other pubs, but this one is always the busiest,' Barry said.

'That's because it has the most atmosphere,' asserted Vicky. 'The others are all modern, but this is sixteenth century.'

'That accounts for the low ceilings,' Jay said, as his head narrowly missed an oak beam. 'They made men smaller in those days!'

'They make most men smaller than you *these* days too!' Vicky smiled. 'It's rather nice to stand next to someone who towers over me.'

'Can't you think of a better reason for enjoying being next to me?' he murmured, as Felice and Barry were distracted by the barmaid asking for their order.

'Frankly? No.'

He chuckled. 'Still determined to go on pretending you're not bowled over by me?'

'You really are the most thick-skinned man I've ever met,' she said crossly. 'Your persistence is beginning to bore me.'

'Women have accused me of many things, but never of boring them.' One dark eyebrow rose higher than the other.

'There's a first time for everything,' she responded coldly.

'If your frigid maiden act is genuine, it's about time you took that saying to heart and did something about it.'

Her cheeks flamed as she understood his meaning. 'Why, you——'

'Anything wrong?' Felice had turned round and noticed the look of fury on her sister's face.

'Yes.' Jay Duncan answered before Vicky could. 'I stepped out of line, and your sister's rightly annoyed with me.'

It was obviously meant as an apology, and, not wishing to make an issue of it, Vicky accepted it as such.

'You're forgiven, Mr Duncan,' she said.

'How about proving it by dispensing with the formalities and calling me Jay?'

Vicky nodded, knowing that for some reason she would find it difficult to say his name. He handed her a drink which, like his own, was a vodka and tonic.

'At least we agree about something,' he smiled.

'As it happens, I dislike the taste of all alcohol except wine, but the wine they serve here is like vinegar.'

'Why choose this, then?'

'Because it tastes of nothing, but has a pleasant effect.'

His eyebrows rose again. 'Pleasant in what way?'

'Not the way *you're* thinking!'

He chuckled, but before he could reply, Barry turned round.

'Anyone fancy crisps or nuts?' he questioned.

'If they've cashews I'll have some,' Felice said. 'I've eaten so much already today, I don't suppose another five hundred calories or so will make much difference.'

'Give me a girl with curves any time.' Jay eyed her appreciatively.

'I'd rather have hair-pin bends like Vicky,' she replied, smiling towards her. 'She eats like a horse and never seems to gain an ounce.'

This led to a discussion on metabolism, an innocuous subject, and Vicky carefully steered the conversation along those lines for the remainder of the evening.

'Will I see you on Saturday?' asked Barry, as he drew to a halt outside the front door of Beauclare's.

'I'm afraid not. Jean's been invited to a wedding, and I have to fill in for her,' Vicky said, naming the cook. At weekends all the food was provided by the school, and with an influx of friends and relations visiting the students and staying for meals, it was an exceptionally busy time.

'Why don't you come and have dinner here?' Felice suggested from the back, much to Vicky's annoyance. If she'd wanted to ask Barry, she would have done so.

'Thanks, but I can't. I've been asked to a twenty-first birthday party, and I was hoping Vicky would come with me.'

'Sorry,' Vicky apologised again. 'But you know how it is during the seminars. We're short-staffed, and everyone has to muck in.'

'Except me, that is,' said Felice. 'I'm treated as though I'm completely incapable.'

'Your talents obviously lie elsewhere,' Jay put in meaningfully.

Felice laughed. 'Give me the chance and I'll show you *where*!' she said shamelessly.

'Sorry, sweetheart, but I don't want to get expelled. I promised your sister I wouldn't break the house rules—and I've a feeling what you have in mind comes into that category!'

'I'll phone you on Friday,' Barry addressed Vicky. 'Perhaps Claudine might take over the evening meal if you explain you have something special on.'

'She's already doing lunch—I can't ask her to do both,' Vicky said with finality.

'I'll ring anyway, just to say hello,' he said resignedly, and kissed her cheek.

'We must do this again,' said Jay with blithe unconcern as he climbed out of the back. 'It's been good fun.'

Vicky was certain it had been no such thing. He was used to the bright lights, and an evening at the local flea-pit, followed by a couple of drinks in a pub, would hardly add up to a 'fun' evening for a sophisticated Man About Town.

Barry did not bother to reply, and with a quick wave of his hand, accelerated down the driveway.

'Your friend's in a bit of a hurry to leave, isn't he?' Jay commented, as he swiftly moved to one side to avoid flying gravel.

'Could be he didn't find the evening as much "fun" as you,' suggested Vicky coolly.

'Could be—though I can't think why.'

The glint in his eyes told her he knew *exactly* why.

'I won't bother to enlighten you.' She turned her key in the lock, and walked in to the hall. 'Are you coming up?' she asked her sister.

Felice looked enquiringly towards Jay, no doubt hoping he would ask her to stay. But when he remained silent, she nodded.

'Goodnight, Jay.'

'Sleep well, Felice—and you too, of course, Vicky,' he added.

Without replying, Vicky moved towards the back staircase.

'What on earth got into you tonight?' her sister asked, hurrying to catch up with her. 'I've never known you so churlish with anyone as you were with Jay.'

Vicky shrugged. 'I just don't happen to like him.'

'But you don't know him.' Felice glanced at her. 'It's not because he fools around in class, is it? Claudine told me about it.'

'Partly.' Vicky grabbed this as a reason. 'But there's also something about him that puts me on edge. He's too good-looking and successful.'

'Just the type I adore! I'm sure if you hadn't been around he'd have asked me to stay.'

'You mean asked you to go to bed with him, don't you?' Vicky said drily.

'And what's wrong with that?' asked Felice defensively. 'I don't believe in playing hard to get, like you—although come to think of it, you don't play at all,' she amended.

'If you mean I'm not a flirt——'

'Too right I do! You never seem to get any fun out of life. You take things far too seriously, instead of letting yourself go and enjoying yourself.'

'You make me sound like a frigid old maid,' Vicky replied.

'You said it, not me.' Felice had clearly wanted to speak her mind for some time, and she was not about to lose the opportunity now. 'As I've told you before, I'm quite capable of taking care of myself and, much as I appreciate your concern for me, I'd rather you stopped trying to tell me how to run *my* life.'

'But the type of life you lead isn't going to end in marriage. That's why I worry about you.'

'There you go again,' Felice sighed with exasperation. 'Can't you get it into your head that men don't expect their wives to be virgins any more when they marry them?' She flung out her hands. 'You sound more like a mother than a sister, and I'm fed up with the way you criticise my friends, my way of life, even my choice of career. Nothing about me seems to please you!'

'Most of it doesn't.' Vicky decided she might as well be equally frank. 'And throwing yourself at *that* man is a very good example of what I mean.'

'*That* man, as you put it, can provide me with my big chance if he chooses me as the Duncan Dolly Bird for his new advertising campaign.'

'I suppose that's why you're here—you knew he would be too, didn't you!'

'And what's wrong if I did?' said Felice defiantly. 'I've not harmed anyone.'

'How did you find out?'

'I know one of the guys who works for his advertising agency. Jay told them he wanted to sit in on all the tests, and they had to know where he was going so they could get hold of him.'

That's what he probably meant in his letter by business commitments, Vicky thought. Nice work, if you could get it!

'I suspected something of the sort,' Vicky said aloud. 'And I don't blame you for taking the opportunity of pushing yourself to the fore—but sleeping with him as part of the deal ...' She shrugged. 'Well, that's another matter.'

'Vicky darling, I'm not a whore—I only sleep with men because I fancy them. If Jay Duncan didn't appeal to me in *that* way, I wouldn't go to bed with him if he promised me my own oil well!'

Unexpectedly, Vicky was close to tears. 'I—I'm sorry, Felice,' she said in a small voice. 'It was a pretty rotten thing to suggest.'

'Apology accepted,' the younger girl said without rancour, and squeezed her sister's arm. 'Now, let's go to bed and forget about Jay Duncan for a while.'

'Good idea—I'm absolutely whacked.'

But sleep did not come easily to Vicky, in spite of fatigue, and finally she switched on the light and read for a while. But, finding it difficult to concentrate sufficiently to absorb the words, she eventually gave up, and put her book aside to lean out of the window and look into the garden. It was a perfect night for star-gazing. Everything was still. Not a blade of grass, not a leaf stirred. There was a full moon and the topiary hedges lining the paths were clearly visible, as was the tall figure of a man moving slowly along one of them. Jay. Had he also had trouble falling asleep, and if so, why? The unusually sultry night, perhaps, or frustration that no one was sharing his bed? It was plain he was finding it difficult to make up his mind whom to proposition, Felice or herself, and was enjoying himself playing one off against the other, even though she had made it quite plain that *her* interest in him was purely professional. But then he was not the kind of man to accept rejection. Probably because he didn't believe she really meant it. He was used to women throwing themselves at him, fawning over him, hanging on to his every word, and no doubt he saw her lack of response as a ploy, a contrivance to hold his attention.

As if she'd compete with her sister! Felice was welcome to him. Or was she? Vicky frowned. In spite of her antipathy towards Jay—no, it was more than that, it was positive dislike—she could not deny that she found him physically attractive. Attractive enough to go to bed with? Surprised she could ask herself such a question about a man she barely knew, she was even more surprised to find that the answer was yes.

The admission hit her hard, like a physical blow, and she recoiled from it with as much fear. What had come over her? Wasn't it against everything she had professed to believe in? Sex without love, without commitment, without emotion of any sort? Believed in? Virginity was not a religion, and losing it hardly amounted to sacrilege.

But could she take a leaf out of Felice's book and put thought into practice? If she tried again and failed in bed with Jay, at least there would be no long-lived embarrassment. No hurt, either. In a few weeks he would disappear from her life, and she would never see him or hear from him again.

But Felice had marked him out for herself, and the last thing Vicky wanted to do was antagonise her sister in any way. She would have to speak to her first before she went ahead. After all, she only wanted Jay Duncan for one night, and then, as far as she was concerned, he was all Felice's, for as long as she could manage to hold him.

CHAPTER SIX

AT seven-thirty the following morning, Vicky knocked on Felice's door. Receiving no reply, she peeped inside and called her sister's name. But when this also failed to elicit a response, she decided on a more brutal approach and roughly drew the curtains aside.

'Surely whatever you needed to say to me could have waited for a less ungodly hour?' the younger girl groaned, burrowing further into the pillows as bright sunlight flooded the room.

'It's not a matter of life and death, if that's what you mean, but I've been up half the night thinking about it, so the least you can do is open your eyes and listen to me,' said Vicky sternly.

'Okay, but only because I smell freshly roasted coffee,' a muffled voice replied. 'Mmm. Hot croissants too,' Felice smiled as she sat up and saw the breakfast tray in Vicky's hands. 'If they're meant as a bribe, you've succeeded. Don't tell me they were made this morning, though?'

Vicky nodded. 'Jean was up and baking at five-thirty, so don't grumble. Compared to her, you're having a lie-in!'

Felice spooned a large dollop of home-made apricot jam on to the golden-brown pastry and bit into it. 'Heavenly,' she sighed contentedly. 'What with breakfast in bed, the sunshine, and Jay Duncan, staying here this time is going to be more of a pleasure than a chore!'

'As it happens, he's the cause of my sleepless night,' Vicky said, perching herself on the end of Felice's bed, and helping herself to a cup of coffee from the pot.

'Not another lecture about him, *please*! I thought we'd agreed on that last night,' her sister said irritably, and then appeared to make a conscious effort to smile. 'One day I'll like a man you won't be able to fault.'

'If he was that perfect, I'd find him a bore!'

'I can't win either way with you, can I!' said Felice. 'But in the meanwhile, in spite of your disapproval, I intend to have as much fun as I can—and that's what you'd be doing too, if you had any sense—as I told you last night!'

'Good advice—I think I'll take it.' Vicky smiled as her answer caused her sister to do a double-take. 'Which is where Jay Duncan comes in—if you don't mind, that is?' she added.

Felice slowly replaced her coffee cup on its saucer, and stared at Vicky in amazement.

'If you mean what I think you mean . . .'

'I do. I've decided to go to bed with him.'

'I seem to remember suggesting you went to bed with *Barry*,' the red-haired girl corrected wryly. 'Anyway, last night you positively loathed the man! What brought on this sudden change of heart?'

'I still positively loathe the man—but like you, I find him fanciable. Which seems to be more important for what I have in mind.'

Felice leaned back against the pillows, a most unladylike whistle emanating from her lips.

'Boy, have *you* grown up overnight!'

'Don't speak too soon. I'm still not sure if I can go

through with it.' Vicky gave a wobbly smile. 'Apart from which, I know you've bagged him for yourself, and I don't want to feel I'm poaching on your territory.'

Felice shrugged. 'Far be it from me to stand in the way of progress! Or to revert to our childhood—I'm quite prepared to share and share alike!'

'There's no need for that,' Vicky assured her hastily. 'I only want him to prove a point. After that, he's all yours.'

'How long do you think it will take you?'

'From the interest he's been showing, I reckon I could manage it before class this morning!' joked Vicky. 'But I don't want to give in too easily, he's conceited enough as it is. Give me a week, and if nothing's happened by then, it means I'm still not ready for it.'

The younger girl giggled. 'If he could only hear you cold-bloodedly planning your own seduction . . .'

'Thank goodness he can't! With an ego his size, it might be a turn-off!'

'I'm no voyeur, but I'd love to be a fly on the wall when you finally succumb.' Felice held up her hand. 'Don't get me wrong. It's the conversation, not the action that interests me—or rather the desire to see if you stop arguing with him long enough to agree to any action!' she qualified. 'I may not have been in love with all the men who've made love to me, but at least I've liked them.'

'Perhaps by the time I go to bed with Jay I may have learned to like him too.'

But somehow Vicky doubted it. Other than his good looks, he had little to recommend him. His business was inherited, though she remembered reading somewhere it had quadrupuled in size since he'd taken over from his father. The point was, could he have made it on his own? Grudgingly she admitted that he was no fool—even though he seemed to enjoy playing the clown when it suited him.

'He's a disruptive influence,' she muttered to herself as she made her way to class, remembering his helpless act of the previous day. No one who'd been in the restaurant business for as long as he had could possibly be as ignorant as he'd pretended. Well, he wouldn't get away with it again. She would make sure he received no help from anyone, and if the end result was inedible, then let him go hungry.

But for the next few days Jay was not only on time for class, but there was a slight improvement in his culinary ability, and though it was unlikely he'd ever be a star pupil, at least he was no longer a disaster area.

However, on Friday he was late once again. Even later than on the first day, and though there were few firm rules at the seminars, one was that everyone arrived on time, to obviate the need for repetition.

'Perhaps you could get up earlier for your swim,' suggested Vicky, deciding that a reprimand of some sort was in order as, begowned and beaming in his pink gingham smock, he sauntered towards her, hands behind his back.

'As it happens I got up an hour and a half earlier,' he replied unperturbed. 'But I drove into Granton to buy you a present, and misjudged how long it would take me.'

With an exaggerated flourish he brought his right arm forward. Nestling in the open palm of his hand was the largest, shiniest Cox's Orange Pippin Vicky had ever seen, gift-tied into a bow, with a white satin ribbon.

'An apple for my teacher.' He smiled winningly, his eyes crinkling at the corners, his mouth curved back to show brilliant white teeth. 'Am I forgiven, or will I still have to stand in the corner?'

Vicky flashed him a look from beneath her lashes. 'Considering your general performance, I think a dunce's cap might be more appropriate!' she replied, amidst the general laughter.

'I'd rather be kept in after school.' His voice was low, the meaning unmistakable.

'We'll settle for perfectly cooked quenelles, Mr Duncan,' Claudine interjected crisply. 'Now, if you'll go to your table so that the ladies can concentrate on Vicky again, she'll continue with the demonstration.'

Although conscious of Jay's eyes upon her, Vicky was too much of a professional to allow it to bother her while she was teaching, and within half an hour her quenelles, light as a feather, were gently simmering in salted water.

'Leave Mr Duncan to me,' Vicky told Claudine after she had instructed the class to begin their own preparations. 'I intend his meal today to be all his own work.'

'You have got it in for the poor man, haven't you?' Claudine said. 'Left to his own devices, I shouldn't think he's capable of boiling a kettle of water, let alone preparing a complicated three-course dinner.' For the first time, the students were being asked to prepare their entire evening meal.

'The only way for him to learn is to be thrown in at the deep end.'

Claudine smiled. 'Well, *chérie*, if he flounders, the

rest of the class will be queuing up to give him mouth to mouth resuscitation!'

With Mrs Smythe-Browne first in line, Vicky thought to herself, as she crossed to the table the woman shared with Jay.

'Would you please allow Jay,'—by now he was on a first-name basis with everyone—'to pound his own pike meat in the mortar? He'll never learn if you insist on doing it for him.'

'He missed that part of the demonstration,' the plump widow replied in an aggrieved tone. 'You can't expect him to guess what to do.'

'He wouldn't have to if he hadn't fooled around and come to class late,' Vicky said.

'Not exactly sweetness and light is she, this morning?' Jay commented to no one in particular. 'Next time I'd better bring her a jar of honey!'

Ignoring the remark, Vicky took the pestle from Mrs Smythe-Browne's hand and held it out towards Jay.

'Wouldn't a food processor be just as good, and save an awful lot of hard work?' he asked, as his table-companion began to pound her own fish.

'The answer is yes to both your questions,' Vicky said. It was his first constructive comment, and a perfectly valid one. 'But the class decided it would be more interesting to make the paste in the traditional way.'

'In that case, far be it from me to go against the majority.'

He set to with such fervour that Vicky would not have been surprised to see the mortar crack in two, but he soon got into a slower rhythm, and she moved away to another table where her help was required to interpret the next part of the recipe.

By four o'clock the class had finished, their efforts temptingly displayed for comment, and with a single exception they were all worthy of praise. The exception, of course, was Jay. If his quenelles were neither the lightest nor the most pleasing shape to the eye, they were at least edible, but the same could not be said for the rest of his meal. His quail—not the largest of birds to start off with—looked as if it had been charcoal-broiled rather than lightly casseroled, and wouldn't have satisfied the appetite of a baby, while the risotto that accompanied it was a sticky mess. As for his Floating Island, this had sunk in a sea of curdled custard, and disappeared without trace!

'I don't seem to be improving, do I?' he asked dispiritedly.

'Don't worry, Jay; we've never had a failure yet,' Claudine assured him cheerfully. 'By the end of the course you'll be looking back on your early efforts and laughing.'

'What do I do in the meantime? Starve to death?' he asked ruefully.

'There's no fear of that,' Vicky interjected. 'Naturally we'll provide you with dinner.'

'I've a better idea. Why don't I provide *you* with dinner instead?' he smiled. The rest of the class had left the room, and other than Claudine and the twins, who were clearing up, they were alone.

'You're certainly not needed here tonight, Vicky,' Claudine prompted encouragingly.

Vicky shrugged. 'In that case I've no excuse for saying no, have I?'

'Would you like to find one?' His tone was humorous.

'Yes—if you intend to take me to a Duncan Diner,' she smiled back. 'I seem to remember you saying you only eat your own fast-food.'

'I'm willing to make an exception tonight,' he answered. 'And believe me, I wouldn't do it for just anyone!'

'We only boast one decent restaurant in Granton.' It was Claudine again. 'And it's difficult to get in at short notice, particularly if they don't know you. Perhaps you'll allow me to book for you?'

'If it's no trouble . . .'

'None—will eight-thirty be all right?' He nodded, and Claudine turned back to Vicky. 'I'll finish up with the girls. Why don't you have a swim?'

'You know what the doctor said—'

'I'll have an early night to make up for it.' Claudine over-rode her protest. 'Now off with you, and enjoy yourself,' she added, with a little push towards the door.

'What's wrong with her?' Jay asked as he followed Vicky out.

'High blood-pressure, and she's inclined to pooh-pooh it.'

'So you act as watch-dog?'

'I have to. Everyone else is afraid of her!'

'I'm sure there's no need to be. Underneath that formidable exterior she's as soft as a marshmallow,' he observed acutely.

'Most people don't realise it, though,' Vicky said, surprised at his acumen.

'I pride myself on being a good judge of character,' he answered casually. 'It's one of the reasons I'm so successful.'

'In business or pleasure?'

'Both,' he answered, so promptly that she laughed.
'Modesty is not your middle name!'

He shrugged. 'I'm only too willing to admit my
faults—so why have false modesty about my virtues?'

They had reached the hall and Vicky halted.
'Because most people confuse honesty with conceit.'

'Brains as well as beauty,' he said admiringly.
'You're wasted here, Vicky.'

'If you're offering to take me out of my life of
hardship and poverty, I accept,' she grinned. 'You're
obviously rich enough to make all my dreams come
true!'

His lids lowered, and it was as if shutters had come
down over his face. 'Is that your only criterion for
happiness?' he asked, a distinct edge to his voice.

'If it were, I wouldn't stick myself down here, would
I?' she countered, surprised by it. 'There aren't many
tycoons hereabouts!'

'What about the fathers of your students? A pretty
girl like you must have attracted their attention.'

It was the second time he'd suggested something of
the sort, and she was irritated by it.

'Where there are fathers there are usually mothers,'
she said coolly.

'My, my,' he mocked. 'You don't smoke, you don't
drink—or at least only in moderation—and you don't
go out with married men. Don't you have any vices?'

Vicky was so angry that it was impossible to speak
calmly. 'None you're ever likely to discover,' she
snapped.

She swung away from him, her cotton skirt swirling
around her, but he caught hold of the material to
prevent her moving away.

'Please let me go,' she said in a tight voice.

'I'm sorry. I guess I overstepped the mark again,' he apologised. 'But only because I like you and want to find out what makes you tick.'

'If you were such a wonderful judge of character, you'd realise it wasn't a diamond-studded Piaget!' She pulled free of him and her heels clicked across the parquet floor.

'I'll see you down by the pool,' he called.

Vicky didn't bother to answer, and went upstairs to change. It would take more than a swim to cool her off and restore her good humour, she thought as she changed into a bikini, choosing her least scanty one and wearing a matching shirt over it. In sapphire-blue silk, it was almost identical with her eyes which were sparkling with anger. She inspected herself in the mirror, remembering Felice's comment about hairpin bends. Was she really too thin? Certainly she had no superfluous fat, but no ribs protruded either, and her breasts, if not *Playboy* centrefold material, were rounded and full enough to have no need of padding.

Why this sudden inventory? Jay Duncan—why pretend otherwise? He infuriated yet attracted her at the same time. Had her anger at his insinuations been unreasonable, perhaps? After all, he was used to a different kind of girl, the kind who rarely wanted a man for himself alone, but rather for what he could do for her or give her. Maybe it had soured him, made him cynical and suspicious, disbelieving in spite of her denials.

The object of her thoughts was already in the pool by the time she went down, a glistening bronzed form, churning through the clear blue water. Expecting to see Felice there, as well as some of the other women, Vicky was surprised to find him alone.

'Join me,' he invited. 'It's glorious.'

Feeling self-conscious, she peeled off her shirt and dived in, forgetting her embarrassment as soon as she entered the water. They splashed around, and swam the length and breadth of the pool, until Clarissa, one of the twins, appeared carrying a tray on which rested an ice-bucket containing a champagne bottle and two glasses.

'You don't mind starting the evening early, do you?' Jay asked, as he climbed lithely out. Skin gleaming as if it had been oiled, hair even blacker now that it was wet, he was a magnificent specimen of manhood.

He did not bother to dry himself, and Vicky noticed that his white briefs made his skin look more bronzed. He had certainly not acquired that colour in English sunshine.

'Marbella,' he answered briefly, when she remarked upon it. 'But topped up here.'

'I was in Marbella a few years ago with a friend,' Vicky said. 'I'd always summered in France before then, but it was the "in" place to be, and we thought we'd take a look and see what all the fuss was about.'

'Did you like it?'

'Very much—we were staying near the port, and spent every evening there, watching the beautiful people on their yachts.'

'None more beautiful than you,' he proclaimed.

To avoid replying, Vicky reached for her towel and patted her shoulders and arms with it, but her hair curled in wet ringlets, and she made no attempt to rub it dry.

'Did you buy this on your trip to Granton this morning?' she asked, noticing the vintage label as he took the champagne out of the bucket. Although they

had a fair wine cellar at Beauclare's, it did not include
the more expensive brands. There was simply no call
for them.

'No, I brought a case of it with me from London—
for emergencies,' he confessed with a grin.

He popped the cork expertly, the powerful biceps in
his arms swelling as he did so.

'Now, tell me all about yourself,' he ordered as he
handed her a glass. 'Where you were born, how you
came to be teaching at Beauclare's, where you worked
before.'

She decided to do exactly as he had asked. If the
questions were meant as a ploy to disarm her, then he
was going to be in for a pretty boring time. But she did
not let her thoughts show on her face as she gave him a
résumé of her life.

'Everything Felice and I have we owe to Claudine.
Our parents were killed in a car crash thirteen years
ago.' She touched lightly on Felice's adoption,
Claudine's relationship with their mother, boarding
school and her sister's decision to pursue her life away
from Beauclare's.

'I can understand your loyalty to Claudine now,' he
said. 'But how come your sister is working down here
if she lives in London?'

Vicky felt herself reddening. 'Finances,' she answered, deciding on a half-truth. 'Hers is a precarious
profession, and I'm afraid that so far her expenses
have outweighed her earnings.'

'With you, no doubt, making up the difference,' he
guessed correctly. 'You strike me as the responsible
type.'

Vicky shrugged off the compliment. 'That's what
big sisters are for.'

'Sense of duty has nothing to do with age. It's something you're born with.'

'Speaking from experience?' she asked casually.

'No—I'm an only child, and one of the fortunate few who've never had to worry about money.' He poured some more champagne and lifted his glass to her. 'Here's hoping the same will one day be true for you.'

At once anger washed over her again. Damn him and his aspersions!

'You seem determined to believe the worst of me, whatever I say to the contrary.' She stood up. 'Perhaps it might be better if we kept our relationship on a pupil-teacher basis.'

Quickly Vicky slipped on her shirt, and, sandals in hand, sped across the grass. But she had only gone a few yards when a hand came out and gripped her shoulder.

'This is the third apology I've had to make to you.'

She turned. 'An apology that's insincere doesn't mean a thing.'

'But I do mean it.' His hand dropped from her shoulder. '*Please*!'

He looked so contrite, it was difficult not to believe him. Or was it just that she wanted to? Preferring not to delve too deeply, she allowed him to lead her back to the poolside.

'I'm surprised we're the only ones here,' Vicky commented as she sat down again on the sun-bed she had just vacated.

'That's by design rather than accident—mine,' Jay told her with a smile. 'I suggested to Felice that she organise a tennis competition, with a couple of bottles of champagne as a prize.'

There was no need to ask why.

'Don't tell me Mrs Smythe-Browne is playing?'

Jay chuckled. 'No—umpiring. Apparently she's been doing so at county level for years.'

'Do you play?' Vicky asked.

He nodded. 'But I prefer squash.'

'Do you belong to a club?'

'I did—until I decided to build my own court in my office block. It was always a hassle having to book in advance, and this way I can play whenever I feel like it.'

'A man of moods?' she questioned.

'No—of too many commitments.'

'Don't you believe in delegating responsibility?'

'To a certain degree I have to. With eight hundred outlets here and in the States, I can't be everywhere at once.' He rubbed the side of his nose. 'But it's essential that everyone working for me believes that I could be. I spend a good deal of my time paying surprise visits.'

'That must involve a lot of travelling,' Vicky commented.

'Of the Wednesday-it-must-be-New-York variety!' he smiled. 'I rarely spend more than a day anywhere— unless I'm on holiday, or at our head office.'

'Or here,' she corrected. 'Unless this counts as a holiday.'

'A working one—but not exactly hard labour.' A big hand came out and rested on her arm, tanned fingers stretched over her skin. 'More a labour of love, I hope,' he added in a low voice.

'Making rather than falling, I assume?'

For an instant he was taken aback at her frankness, and then the tightness left his face and was replaced by a grin.

'I always fall for the women I make love to—does that answer your question?'

'No—but it's a good answer!'

He chuckled. 'I like your honesty—it's refreshing.'

'So is your flirting,' she responded. 'You may never master the art of cooking, but there's nothing you need to learn about handing out a line!'

'I thought that was your forte—teacher!' His fingers tightened on her arm.

It was spoken lightly, yet she sensed there was more to it, like much of what he said. Yet what could there be?

'That's something I'd never do,' she answered, deciding to take the comment seriously. 'I always thought lines were a ridiculous punishment, even when *I* was at school.'

Jay released her arm, and leaned back in his chair, squinting his eyes against the sun. 'What's the best way of controlling a class, then?'

'Holding their interest—and that applies to whatever age group you're teaching.'

'That may work in theory, but in a deprived area, among a group of slum kids . . .'

'As part of my training, I worked for a term in a large comprehensive in Oxton.' Vicky named a town with notoriously high unemployment. 'At first I was treated as something of a joke—middle-class accents don't go down too well in that part of the world. But once they realised I was on their side, and not just patronising them, I was surprised by their response.'

'You sound as if you enjoyed it.'

'I did—enough to make me want to go back there when I'd finished my training.'

'What swayed you? That sense of duty again?'

Vicky nodded. 'Claudine's always seen me as her successor, and I knew she'd be broken-hearted.'

'She's still quite young, though, so her retirement's a long way off. In the meanwhile you might marry.'

'If it's someone from round here, I could still run the school of course.'

'And if it's not?' he prompted. 'Or is it conditional?'

'Of course not,' she answered decisively. 'But as I live here for eleven months of the year, it's certainly a probability.'

'Don't you believe in holiday romances?' asked Jay.

'Since the age of fifteen, when I fell for our hotel waiter, who was married with five children, I can't say I've had one! Dates, of course, but if you're the kind of girl who doesn't want to end up in bed paying for them, they tend to be one-off evenings.'

'Are you frigid or just fussy?'

Vicky's first reaction was one of anger, but it died as swiftly as it had come when she saw from his grin that this time he was teasing her.

'I'm definitely fussy, but as for being frigid . . .' Deliberately she stopped, dangling the sentence in mid-air, like a worm in front of a fish.

Jay smiled, but thought better of pursuing the bait.

'I guess that question didn't deserve an answer!' he said, then glanced at his watch, lying on the white-slatted table between them. 'Nearly six. Do you fancy another swim before we go up to change?'

'Not really—but don't let me stop you.'

He padded to the side of the pool. Soft-footed as a panther, and equally sleek and dangerous, he executed a perfect dive that left her gasping with envy, then ploughed cleanly through the water, length after length, until, feeling her eyes grow heavy, Vicky lost count of the number, and shut her eyes.

The sound of a man's voice brought her back to consciousness. She opened her eyes and cautiously looked around her. It was Jay's, though he was not aware of it, as he was fast asleep in the chair next to her. Not wishing to disturb him, she carefully raised herself on one elbow and looked at him. Relaxed, he appeared a different man, younger, though in no way weaker. What a curious mixture he was; one moment aggressive, the next contrite, one moment teasing, the next serious. As he lay there with his eyes closed she realised that his lashes were long and thick enough to be the envy of any girl, his brow wide and serene. His hair was untidy and still damp, and because of the way he was lying, fell across his forehead. She felt an urge to feel the texture between her fingers, to push it away from his face . . .

'Like what you see?'

Vicky gave a startled jerk. 'I didn't realise you were awake,' she said sheepishly.

'Obviously,' he replied drily. 'But you haven't answered my question.'

'You'll do,' she said, matter-of-factly.

'Not exactly erudite, but better than plain no!' Jay shifted and pulled himself up into a sitting position. 'It's unusual for me to fall asleep like that,' he smiled. 'And certainly not my usual behaviour when I'm lying next to a beautiful girl.'

She felt the colour run under her skin, and was conscious of his amusement. 'I'll take that as a warning,' she said, putting on her sandals.

'There's still some champagne left,' he said as she stood.

'That's what made me feel sleepy,' Vicky told him.

'If you want me alert during dinner, then don't tempt me to more.'

'More what?' he asked guilelessly.

Knowing he did not expect a reply, she merely smiled.

'I'll meet you in the hall at eight,' he said. 'Claudine's booked the table for half-past, and it shouldn't take more than twenty minutes to get there.'

Vicky arched her eyebrows. 'Flying or driving?'

He laughed. 'My car's a bit faster than Barry's.'

'You mean your driving is!'

'Don't worry. I've never had an accident yet.'

'Neither have I. It's always the other person's fault!'

He laughed again. 'If you need reassuring, the last time I had a crash was in my pedal-car when I was five years old!'

CHAPTER SEVEN

THERE was still heat in the sun as Vicky crossed the lawns to the long flagged terrace, though the shadows were lengthening as it moved behind the house, bathing the cream stone in a mellow light that gave it a golden hue. There was a springiness in her step that had not been there two hours ago on the way down to the pool. She did not want to analyse this sudden lift to her spirits for fear she would read either too much or too little into it, thereby spoiling the moment. Certainly her opinion of Jay had changed somewhat, her interest in him was aroused beyond the physical.

Back in her room, Vicky surveyed her dresses. She would like to have worn something more 'with it' than her turquoise and white silk, aware that, compared to the glamorous and sophisticated women Jay was used to, she would appear very much the country bumpkin. In spite of its flattering line and colour, it was far from *haute couture*! If only she and Felice were nearer the same shape, it would solve all her problems. Her sister's wardrobe—purchased mainly in sales, it was true—was full of high-fashion labels. Still, Jay had not been attracted to her because of her clothes. The day he'd arrived she had looked as if she'd been dragged through a hedge backwards in her washed-out cotton skirt and T-shirt. It was the body beneath the clothes that interested him. The face too, of course—and, if her intuition had not led her astray and made her unduly hopeful, the mind behind it as well.

There was no time to set her hair, and she let it wave

loosely round her head, unaware that the style enhanced her fragility, and made her look younger than her years.

Jay was waiting for her as she came down the stairs, leaning casually against the banisters as he watched her. He was dressed in brown trousers and jacket of impeccable cut, with a cream silk shirt and a striped tie in the same two colours. As she came level with him he linked his arm with hers, and led her out to the scarlet Ferrari, parked near the front door.

'You certainly couldn't lose this in a crowded car park!' she joked as they set off.

'That's why I chose such a bright colour—though with thieves in mind rather than parking. Even the dullest bobby on the beat wouldn't have any difficulty spotting it if it were stolen.'

'It could be re-sprayed, though.'

'I was thinking more of kids joy-riding. That's on the increase, and in a way even worse. They tend to vandalise the cars so badly that it's not always possible to put them right again.'

Vicky smiled, thinking of her ten-year-old Mini. 'I think they've already been at work on my car without my knowing it!'

As she had expected, Jay handled the Ferrari with ease, and though occasionally conscious of his fingers accidentally brushing against her thigh as he changed gear, she was able to relax, leaning back in the comfortable black leather seat, and watching the hedgerows that lined the narrow lane flash by. With two minutes to spare out of the twenty he had estimated, he swung into the car park of the Jolly Miller.

'All in one piece, as promised,' he smiled as he helped her out.

The bar was so crowded that there was no place to sit down, and Jay suggested they went straight to their table and had an aperitif there.

'I'd sooner just have wine with my dinner, if you don't mind,' Vicky answered.

'Still feeling the effects of the champagne?' he questioned.

She nodded. 'It's given me a slight headache.'

'I thought that excuse generally came *after* the meal!' he teased.

'I don't need excuses, Jay. I just say *no*, loud and clear!'

He chuckled. 'Always?'

Vicky picked up the menu. 'Sorry, but I never play true confessions on an empty stomach!'

Acknowledging her adroit handling of the question with a wry smile, Jay concentrated on choosing his meal.

Surprisingly, when they came to order, their tastes proved identical; soupe aux truffes, and rack of lamb with herbs, cooked pink in the French manner.

'I expected you to ask for bubble and squeak or steak and kidney pudding,' Vicky commented, when the waiter had departed. 'I seem to remember that's the kind of fare you serve in your restaurants.'

'I guess I'll never live that remark of mine down, will I?' he smiled. 'But I only said it to make my point. I didn't mean it to be taken literally.'

'Do you employ a cook at home?'

'If I didn't I'd be a walking advert for Famine Relief, wouldn't I?' he grinned. 'But I actually employ two. One in London, and one in Marbella, where I have a villa and a yacht.'

'Yacht?' she repeated. 'I've never met anyone who actually owned one.'

'Impressed?'

Once again she sensed an undercurrent, but his expression was so artless that she decided she'd imagined it.

'Madly,' she answered drily. 'How many does it sleep?'

'Eight, plus a crew of three.'

'It must be quite a size.'

'Large enough to land a helicopter on the deck—though no one's actually tried!' he added.

'You obviously haven't the right friends!' she smiled.

'I have, but they're all into Lear jets this year!'

'You too?' she asked.

'I make do with Concorde!'

'Slumming it a bit, aren't you? What *will* people say?'

He chuckled. 'I'm too rich to care!'

Their soupe aux truffes arrived, and the waiter deftly broke the flaky pastry covering the bowls, so that it fell into the soup.

'Well, they certainly serve it properly,' Jay observed, when they were alone again. 'But whether it will taste as good as the Roux brothers' is another matter.'

'Reading Albert's cookery book is the nearest I've been to his restaurant,' Vicky said, 'so you'll have to be the arbiter.'

She watched while Jay tasted it, a smile of satisfaction crossing his face.

'Not bad,' he murmured. 'A few more truffles and some extra foie gras wouldn't go amiss, but that's all.'

Vicky was impressed. 'You may not be able to cook, but you're knowledgeable about the ingredients,' she remarked.

'Only the odd thing,' he said quickly. 'When it's really unusual I make a point of finding out what went into it, so my chef can make it.

'Now you know why it's so difficult to get in here,' Vicky said. 'They've had excellent write-ups in all the food guides, with the exception of Mark Mason. Strangely enough, he doesn't mention it.'

'Perhaps he doesn't know about it,' surmised Jay, his head turned away from her to call the wine waiter.

'As he professes to be the High Priest of the guide books, that's not a very valid excuse. He *should* know about it!'

'Why don't you write and tell him?' Jay suggested.

'I already have—but he didn't deign to reply. I even mentioned that I worked at Beauclare's, and Claudine penned a note to give added weight to the recommendation.'

'Obviously his publisher didn't pass it on to him,' he said defensively.

Vicky was amused. 'You men certainly stick together, don't you! If I'd been talking about a woman you'd probably make some crack about her reputation having gone to her head, and being too full of her own importance to bother with letters from the hoi-polloi.'

'I'd hardly put you and Claudine in *that* category, even if your allegation was true. And as for Mark Mason, I know he's always willing to take up recommendations from the public and investigate them. I—er—I read it somewhere,' he explained, somewhat falteringly, in answer to her questioning look.

'From the way you're defending him I'm beginning to think you're related!' Vicky teased, and leaned forward conspiratorially. 'Perhaps you're even here on his behalf!'

'Of course,' he agreed humorously. 'And I'm using my disguise as the world's worst cook to fool you!'

Their main course arrived, and they remained silent until their glasses had been filled with the claret Jay had chosen.

'This is excellent,' said Vicky appreciatively as she tasted it. 'I normally don't drink red wine, but when I heard what you were ordering, I had to taste it.'

'Good wine is inbred in me,' Jay told her with a smile. 'My mother's Italian, and her family are in the business. They own a vineyard in Tuscany, and bottle under their own label. I spent many happy working holidays there in my youth.'

So I was right, Vicky thought. He did have Latin blood in him.

'Would I have heard of it?' she asked aloud.

'I imagine so—Boltucello.'

Vicky nodded. The name was famous.

'They have it on the wine list here, I noticed,' Jay continued. 'And if you're wondering why I didn't order it, it's not because I think it's inferior to French in any way, it's just that I feel French food is best complemented by French wine.'

'By that reckoning, you'd only serve English wine in your restaurants.'

'If I could I would,' he agreed. 'Unfortunately, as you probably know, it's produced in comparatively small quantities, and we could never get enough.'

Vicky nodded again. 'We have a vineyard near here, and a tour on the Tuesday of your third week is part of the curriculum.'

'With you as guide, I hope?'

'No—that's one of Felice's jobs.'

'In that case, if everyone else is going and you're free that day, why not spend it giving me a tour of the

countryside instead?' Jay suggested. 'Having wine in
my veins, so to speak, a tour round a vineyard is the
last thing I need.'

Vicky frowned. 'Tuesday is Barry's day off, and I'd
intended to spend it with him. It's one of the few
opportunities I'll have until the course finishes.'

'If your conscience needs easing, call it extra
tuition—for which privilege, may I remind you, I'm
paying handsomely.' He accompanied this with a
smile to show there was no sting implied. 'On my own
you'll find I'm the perfect pupil; good-natured,
attentive and extremely obedient.'

'You sound like Tara, our Red Setter!' Vicky
smiled.

'Then agree to go out with me. You know what they
say about being kind to dumb animals?'

'I also know what they say about every dog having
its day,' she countered. 'I hope you're not planning on
having yours on Tuesday!'

Jay burst out laughing. It was a warm, uninhibited
sound, and she was hard put to it not to join in. But
resolutely she didn't, and stared down at her plate
until he was silent.

'Frightened you'll succumb to my undoubted
charms?' he asked.

'Of course.' She gave him the full battery of her eyes.
'You're the best-looking man I've met, and as a bonus
you're rich and single. What more could any girl
want?'

The look he gave her was sharp, as if trying to
decide if she meant it or was joking again. He was
about to answer, when she saw his eyes move to a
point above her head.

'I think we have company,' he murmured.

'Shortage of food at Beauclare's?' The question was

Barry's, as was the hand on her shoulder.

'No. Just a case of one of the cooks spoiling his broth!' Jay answered before Vicky could.

'And I suppose you hate dining alone, so you asked Vicky to take pity on you,' added Barry sarcastically.

'Something like that,' came the smooth reply.

Barry stared down at Vicky, the gleam in his eyes definitely not one of amusement.

'Who are you with?' asked Vicky brightly into the silence.

'Ann,' he answered briefly, then for the other man's benefit added somewhat sourly, 'My partner.'

Jay's eyes strayed to a table in the far corner of the room, where a blonde girl sat on her own.

'If that's her, you're a lucky guy. Partners don't usually come packaged so prettily.'

'I chose Ann for her qualifications, not her looks,' said Barry stiffly. 'And our relationship is strictly business.'

Jay didn't reply, but his sceptical look spoke volumes.

'Why don't you join us for coffee when you're finished?' Vicky suggested, in an effort to avoid pistols at dawn.

'I doubt if we'll still be here,' Jay said, glancing down at the narrow sliver of gold on his wrist. 'I'm expecting a business call at eleven-thirty.'

'Rather late in the day for business,' Barry stated questioningly.

'I could say the same for you, old chap,' answered Jay with a quick look in the direction of Barry's partner.

Barry reddened and, conscious of the tension mounting between the two men with every word,

Vicky racked her brains for something to say that would ease it.

'I'll phone you tomorrow evening.' She addressed Barry with a warm smile. 'Perhaps we can get together some time on Sunday—if you're free, that is?'

'I'll make sure I am,' he answered, brightening considerably. Then, with a cursory nod at Jay, he squeezed her shoulder gently and moved away.

'I get the feeling he doesn't like me,' Jay proclaimed as soon as he was out of earshot.

'Could be he didn't believe your excuse about the telephone call,' replied Vicky.

'Could be he was right not to,' said Jay unrepentantly. 'Unless it's business or family, I prefer not to share my dinner companions. I like to concentrate on them alone.'

'Frightened of the competition?' Vicky mocked.

'You know better than that,' he smiled. 'Anyway, after seeing you and Barry together, I don't regard him as competition.'

'Then you're wrong. I'm very fond of him.'

'*Fond*?' repeated Jay. 'That's a word reserved for friends, not lovers.'

'It's possible to be both, surely?'

He shook his head. 'Not in my experience.'

'Then you've never been in love.'

'Fortunately not. It's a complication I can live without.'

'Why a complication?'

'Because love spells permanency of some kind or another, and I have no desire to settle down.'

'That's because you haven't met the right girl,' Vicky asserted.

'I seem to have heard *that* somewhere before!' He gave her a slow, appraising look. 'Of course, there's always a chance *you* could be Miss Right and change my mind.'

'That's presupposing I see you as *Mr* Right!'

'There's a good way of finding out, isn't there?'

His glance caressed her, and she felt herself growing warm.

'Dessert, Miss Marshall?'

The welcome interruption of the sweet trolley saved Vicky from answering, and she deliberately spent some time deciding what to have. But Jay was not put off in the least, and returned to the attack as soon as he had made his own choice.

'You intrigue me, Vicky. You're a bright girl, never at a loss for an answer, yet any reference to sex makes you blush like an innocent sixteen-year-old.'

She wondered what he would say if she told him she was an innocent twenty-four-year-old. Probably drop me like a hot potato, she decided. He was not looking to initiate a novice, but to alleviate the boredom of the long evenings with a girl of experience. For all he had hinted that she could be Miss Right, it meant nothing, and was all part of the game—the game of getting her into bed. Sexually uninitiated she might be, but her naïveté stopped there.

'Don't forget I'm a simple country girl, unused to the bluntness of city slickers,' she said aloud.

Jay smiled, remembering he had used the term to describe himself.

'A country girl you may be, but simple you're not!'

'In the broadest sense of the word I am,' she argued. 'I'm reasonably well travelled, and I've lived for a time in a city, but I don't think I would ever want to make my home in one permanently.'

'So marriage has to be a mansion in the country?'

'A rose-covered cottage was more what I had in

mind,' Vicky said. 'Not that I've anything against marrying money,' she added. 'But that usually means an older man——'

'Not necessarily. I know quite a few young millionaires.'

'But how many do you know who marry girls like me? They tend to stick to their own kind.'

'What makes an older man different?' Jay enquired.

'He controls his own purse-strings, rather than his parents, and though he knows his nymphet is settling for gold rather than love, he's prepared to convince himself otherwise, because he can't get her any other way.'

'That's a very cynical attitude,' Jay commented. 'Speaking from experience?'

'Not my own—my sister's.' He looked surprised and she elaborated, cataloguing Felice's various misadventures.

'She's obviously attracted to the wrong type,' observed Jay when she had finished. 'What you've told me may have applied at one time, but all this talk of class is a load of claptrap. It doesn't matter today what people have or even inherit; it's what you *are* that counts.'

'Money is still inclined to marry money,' disagreed Vicky firmly. 'And in spite of what you say, I'm sure when you decide to take the plunge it will apply to you too.'

'I can't give you any guarantee one way or another, as I'm not sure if I've met my one and only. But lack of money or her antecedents won't influence my *choice*. *That* I can say categorically.'

'I'll watch out for the announcement in *The Times*.'

'Disbelieving type, aren't you?'

Vicky shrugged, and Jay made no further comment. He beckoned for the bill and checked it thoroughly before extracting a credit card from a black crocodile-skin card-holder. She noticed that he added an extremely generous tip, and felt a warm glow of satisfaction. He might be used to more glamorous restaurants, but it showed he was more than satisfied with the meal he'd eaten here.

Afterwards they drove slowly home, to the accompaniment of a Marvin Hamlisch cassette, played on the piano by the composer himself.

As the melodic strains wafted around them, Vicky's lids closed, and she lay back against the black hide of her seat. How supple it felt, reminding her fancifully of Jay's body as he had churned through the water in the pool this afternoon.

The cessation of movement as the car stopped awoke her, and she found she had fallen against Jay's shoulder. His arm was acting as a support, and her hair was spread across his jacket. Frightened of his nearness, she tried to move away, but he nuzzled his face into her hair, and drew her closer. With an effort she forced herself to relax, and he gave a murmur of contentment, pulling her tightly against him, moulding her body to his.

'You're as soft as a kitten,' he said huskily.

'But not nearly as playful!' she quipped softly, and with a sudden movement, pulled away from him.

She heard him chuckle as she opened the car door, but he made no reply as he came round to help her out. In spite of her height, Jay topped Vicky by a good few inches, and she felt small and defenceless beside him as they walked up the steps of the house and into the hall.

'It's been a lovely evening,' she murmured politely,

and turned towards the back staircase.

But he caught hold of her arm and stopped her, pulling her close to him. She felt the hardness of his frame down the length of her, and the steely strength of his thighs pressing her own.

'Then why end it so early?' he questioned thickly. 'You've fallen asleep on me twice, so you can't be feeling tired.'

'That was the wine,' she said. 'If I stay up late, I find it difficult to sleep.'

'What I had in mind is very relaxing,' he whispered, his breath warm against her ear. 'Can't you tell how much I want you, Vicky?'

The knowledge that she had aroused him gave her little satisfaction. How could it, when she knew that any attractive face would have the same effect? He was a born womaniser.

'I prefer not to mix business with pleasure.' Vicky forced herself to remain inert against him, in the hope that he would let her go. 'I thought I'd already made that clear.'

'I thought normal rules didn't apply to me!'

'Only regarding cookery tuition. For what you have in mind, I suspect you already have an honours degree!'

'I'm quite happy to switch roles and teach you a few things!'

She tried to think of a flippant reply, but for once was at a loss. His nearness, the feel of his skin, the heat radiating from his body, his throbbing need, were making it increasingly difficult for her to stay cool. Slowly her own limbs were melting, her own heart pulsating as fast as his, while a moistness suffused her that had little to do with the sultriness of the evening.

Only a determination not to make his conquest too

easy for him stopped her from giving in. She would go on playing hard to get for a little while longer. If he wanted her enough he would persist—and if he didn't? Well, she was prepared to take the risk, though there was no denying she would be disappointed.

'My reply still stands,' she said with commendable coolness. 'And I'm beginning to find your persistence tedious. Can't you understand that not every girl wants to jump into bed with you, and that when some say no, they mean it?'

She heard him catch his breath sharply, but he gave no other sign of anger. Gently, he released her.

'No one's ever said it to me before,' he said quietly. 'But, as I told you earlier, I'm a quick learner. Meanwhile, don't try and wriggle out of our Tuesday date. I intend to hold you to it.'

She shrugged. 'My time is yours—during daylight hours at least!'

'Then it's a pity we're not in the land of the midnight sun!'

Deciding to award him the victory of the last word, she remained silent.

'I'll say *au revoir*, then,' he went on. 'Just in case I don't see you in the morning.'

'Why shouldn't you?' she said. 'I'm not going anywhere.'

'But I am,' he answered. 'As you're not going to be available at the weekend, I think I'll spend it in London.'

'The idea of free weekends is for friends and family to visit *you*,' she pointed out. 'It makes for an informal and relaxed atmosphere, with everyone mixing and getting to know one another.'

'The only person I'm interested in getting to know better won't be around,' he answered. 'Unless you

change your mind about seeing Barry on Sunday, of
course? Then I might decide to stay.'

Vicky shook her head. 'You really are irrepressible,
Jay.'

'I'll take that as no, shall I?' he drawled.

It was impossible to keep a straight face, and
chuckling, she turned on her heel and went quickly up
the stairs.

Back in her room, Vicky's laughter died. She had
not been entirely honest with herself about her reason
for turning Jay down tonight. Her refusal was not
solely because she wanted to knock some of the
conceit out of him by continuing to show indifference.
Spending time with him had only confirmed how
much more there was to him than good looks and a
quick line in repartee. He used his devil-may-care
image to mask the more serious side of his nature—the
success he had achieved by working for himself rather
than resting on his father's laurels testified to that as
much as anything else.

Why he assumed this role she did not know.
Perhaps it was to cover a guilt complex at having had
things too easy, being blessed with all the gifts of the
gods. Whatever, he intrigued her. If, by delaying her
seduction, she could go on holding his interest, and
make him see her as something more than a pleasing
interlude, then who could tell how their relationship
might develop?

So where did that leave her? Rather like Oliver
Twist, she concluded finally. Wanting more, but
knowing that getting it was probably wishful
thinking.

CHAPTER EIGHT

EXPECTING a barrage of questions, Vicky was surprised when, by ten o'clock the next morning, curiosity had not roused Felice from her bed.

'She's not there.' Jean, the cook, was coming out of her own room and saw Vicky knocking on her sister's door. 'She left with Mr Duncan at eight,' the girl continued. 'I hope I'm not telling tales out of school,' she half smiled at her unintentioned pun, 'but I'm not surprised. I was up early, and caught him leaving her room.'

So if Jay couldn't have one sister, he'd made sure of the other, Vicky thought instantly, and felt a sharp stab of emotion she could not analyse. So much for all his talk about *her* being special, and so much for all her fantasising that she might be! He was nothing but a flirt who liked to play the field. What other explanation could there be for him sleeping with Felice last night, and persuading her to go to London with him for the weekend? Not that she had probably needed much persuading. She had made no bones about finding her duties both arduous and boring, and it was typical of her to just get up and go, without thought of how it would affect anyone else's arrangements—particularly Vicky's own, as the brunt of extra work would fall on her. There was no way she could spend any time alone with Barry now—though the thought did not upset her as much as make her feel guilty.

To ease her conscience, she immediately telephoned

him, and asked him over for Sunday lunch.

'I was hoping to see you alone,' he said, obviously disgruntled.

'I know—but there's nothing I can do about it. You know how short-handed we are, and with Felice taking off like that——'

'That chap's an absolute bounder—I could tell as soon as I met him he spelled trouble,' Barry grumbled.

Vicky could not help smiling at Barry's description of Jay. It conjured up a picture of a moustachioed villain in a Victorian melodrama, rather than a twentieth-century jet-setter.

'How typically irresponsible!' Claudine sighed, when she heard the news of Felice's flight.

'I blame Jay just as much.' Vicky did not try to hide her anger at what she could not help thinking of as some kind of personal betrayal.

'I don't see why,' answered Claudine. 'Felice made it very obvious she fancied him, and he took advantage of it. I suppose you turned him down last night, didn't you?'

'What do you mean?' Vicky asked innocently.

Claudine smiled. 'Don't tell me he didn't ask you to go to bed with him?'

'You're an old witch, do you know that?'

'Neither old, nor a witch!' Claudine chuckled. 'I know the kind of man Jay is, and I know the kind of girl you are.'

'Funnily enough, I'd made up my mind to accept if he asked me,' Vicky confided, and went on to more or less repeat the conversation she had had with Felice on the same subject.

'It shows how innocent you really are, if you thought your refusal would undermine Jay's self-confidence,' Claudine commented when she had finished. 'Or is there more to it?' she added shrewdly.

Vicky smiled. 'Okay, mind-reader, I'll confess all. I fell for his line, and hoped that by refusing I'd hold his interest a while longer, and he'd begin to see me as something other than just a pretty face.'

'Unlike your sister, you need to be wanted for your mind as well as your body,' Claudine said drily, encapsulating Vicky's feelings accurately. She nodded, and the Frenchwoman continued, 'What will you do next time he asks you?'

'Who says there'll be a next time?'

'If he hadn't preferred you in the first place, he would have bedded Felice his first night here,' came the answer. 'He's merely using her as a convenience, but on Monday, I'm willing to bet anything he'll turn his attention back to you.'

'Somehow it seems tacky to share a guy with one's sister,' said Vicky.

'But you were going to do that anyway,' the older woman pointed out correctly.

Vicky sighed heavily. 'I know—but being first was different.'

'Personally I don't see it—but of course it's up to you.'

By Monday morning Vicky was still undecided what to do should Claudine's prediction concerning Jay turn out to be correct. She'd barely had time to think at the weekend, and had been so tired that she had fallen asleep as soon as her head touched the pillow. The weather had stayed hot and sultry, and being stuck in the kitchen most of Saturday did little to keep her good-humoured. Even Barry, who was generally easy going, and took little notice if she was in a bad mood, left before tea on Sunday.

'You're really out of sorts,' he remarked, as she

accompanied him to his car. 'You've acted like a bear with a sore head the whole afternoon.'

'I'm sorry,' she said, genuinely contrite. 'I'll make it up to you next time I see you.'

'When will that be?' he pounced immediately.

'I'm not sure yet.'

'In other words, don't phone me, I'll phone you!' he answered drily.

For answer, Vicky kissed him resoundingly on the mouth. It was not a kiss of passion though, but one of thanks for his tolerance, and, sensing it, he himself did not attempt to make anything more of it, merely squeezing her hand and then getting into his car.

'Have a good time?' Vicky asked, when her sister joined her at breakfast. Claudine had already seen Felice and told her what she thought of her in no uncertain terms, so there was no point in going over the same ground. But she was still seething at Felice's careless and unthinking behaviour, and it took a great effort not to show it.

'Marvellous!' The younger girl's eyes sparkled, and there was no hint of contrition in her voice.

'I hear you got what you wanted.' Claudine had already conveyed the news that Felice had been chosen as the new Duncan Dolly Bird for Jay's advertising campaign.

'For once—yes!'

'You must have really given satisfaction to get things settled so quickly.' It sounded bitchy, but Vicky couldn't stop herself.

Felice appeared unaware of it though, and smiled. 'Jay told me I was by far the best,' she said matter-of-factly. 'It seems I'm a natural.'

'You've had a lot of experience,' commented Vicky drily.

'Not compared to the other girls.'

'You mean there were several of you?' Vicky asked in shocked disbelief. Even with Felice's casual approach to sex, this was going to far.

'How could he know who was the best if he didn't try us all?' the girl replied shamelessly. 'And they were all as lovely as me,' she added. 'I think it was my red hair that finally swung things my way.'

'I was always under the impression gentlemen preferred blondes,' said Vicky sarcastically. 'But then, of course, Jay Duncan is no gentleman.'

'I have to disagree with you there, but no doubt he'll tell you all about the weekend himself. He talked a good deal about you.' Felice gave a short laugh. 'Hardly flattering, I may say, but I didn't care once I had the contract in my pocket and found out how much I'd be earning.' She leaned across the table and covered Vicky's hand with her own. 'I'll be able to pay you back all I owe you, and more besides. I want you to share my good fortune—you've sacrificed a good deal to help me, and the least I can do is buy you an extravagant present.'

While she had not expected an abject apology from Felice about breaking her promise and sleeping with Jay first, the girl's blind assumption that it meant nothing to her irritated Vicky, and only the entrance of Clarissa, one of the twins, with her own breakfast, stopped her from commenting on it.

'That's nice of you,' Vicky answered coolly. 'But I'll be happy just to get back what you owe me. Now I won't have to finance you, I'll be able to afford to buy myself whatever I want, within reason.'

'Won the pools, have you?' asked Clarissa curiously, grinning at Felice.

'Something like that,' Felice replied, and began to regale the young girl with the details as she tucked in to her cornflakes.

'Excuse me,' murmured Vicky, and stood up. 'I have things to prepare for class.'

It was only partly true, for whatever needed doing could have waited another half an hour, but disgust with her sister, and the need to suppress her own anger, made it difficult for her to stay in the same room. No doubt I'll have calmed down by lunchtime, she mused as she entered the demonstration kitchen where today's lesson on boning and stuffing meat and poultry was to take place—and by this evening I will, as usual, have completely forgiven Felice. The girl's own good humour made it difficult to stay cross with her for long. But how was she going to feel towards Jay when she saw him again? Vicky wondered. Would her attraction to him be as strong or would his weekend with Felice have dimmed her interest in him?

'Hello.' The man on her mind smiled at her from the far end of the room.

The sight of his tall figure, casually dressed in short-sleeved shirt and tight jeans that clung to long muscular legs, answered her question, for she began to tremble in the most foolish way. It was only two days since she had last seen him, yet it was all she could do not to stare at him. Instead she kept her eyes on the wall oven that rose behind one broad, white cotton-covered shoulder.

'Lessons don't begin for another hour,' she stated frigidly.

'No one knows that better than me.' His tone was humorous. 'And that's why I'm here.'

'I've work to do,' she said unbendingly. 'You'll have to excuse me.'

Vicky went to move past him, but he caught her arm.

'If your tone is anything to go by I think I'd better begin by apologising—just for a change.'

'Really? Whatever for?' she asked with deliberate innocence.

'You know damn well.' His voice was suddenly rough, as was his hold as he gripped her. 'You're annoyed with me because of Felice.'

'Your time is your own, and so is what you do with it.'

'I didn't realise until we were driving home last night that she wasn't free to come with me, or that she hadn't even bothered leaving a note explaining things.'

Vicky shrugged. 'It doesn't matter one way or another. Obviously your ego needs both of us. In spite of what you said about wanting me, you wanted her as well.'

'That's not true!' he denied angrily. 'I admire her looks, but she doesn't turn me on. Not the way you do,' he added quietly.

'No doubt if I'd spent the weekend with you, you'd be saying the same thing to Felice about *me*.' She threw back her head and stared at him defiantly. 'You obviously have a low threshold of boredom.'

'You think I want both of you?' Jay asked in amazement. 'You *and* Felice?'

'After what's happened, I'd hardly call it surprising,' she retorted scathingly.

'But I just told you I didn't know she'd taken off without a word.'

'And that's supposed to make everything all right, is it?' she demanded.

'Well, there's nothing else to be sore about. Unless you're jealous that she's landed the contract?'

'That's a lousy thing to suggest!' Vicky cried. 'I'm thrilled for her! It's what she had to do to get it that I object to.'

'If you're suggesting what I think you're suggesting . . .' He gave her a hard stare. 'Well, well. So that's what this is really all about.'

'Don't flatter yourself,' she flared. 'I'm not jealous of that either.'

'Then what the hell are you so angry about?' he grated. 'I didn't lay a hand on Felice—or at least, not in the way you seem to think—and if she told you anything different, she's lying.'

'Why should she?'

'I'm afraid I don't know enough about your relationship to answer that.'

'Felice would lie about a lot of things, but not sex. It isn't important enough to her.'

'Nor to me.' He pushed her none too gently away from him. 'I took Felice to London solely because she's been angling for a Duncan Dolly Bird test from the first day I came here. I knew the agency were viewing some girls on Saturday, and as you were busy, it seemed like a good opportunity to ask Felice along and get her out of my hair once and for all.' His voice was deep, but without expression. 'As things turned out, the agency agreed with me that she was perfect for the job, and it was pointless to go on searching further. My lawyer works a six-day week, and he drew up a contract then and there.' Jay looked at her, his eyes narrowed by the dark brows lowered over them. 'Believe me or not, that's all there was to it.'

Vicky thought back to the conversation she'd had with her sister. At no time had Felice actually said she'd slept with Jay to get the contract. Knowing she was prepared to do so, Vicky had simply assumed it. Everything Jay had just told her tied in with what she'd already heard—and completely misinterpreted after Jean had confided that she'd seen him coming out of her sister's bedroom.

What a fool she'd made of herself, and how stupidly she'd behaved. Giving way to her anger, she had also given away her feelings, and had allowed him to see that she cared more than she had pretended. He was too experienced with women to be fooled by any attempt at a denial now.

'I'm sorry,' she said aloud. 'Jean saw you coming out of Felice's bedroom early on Saturday morning, and I assumed you'd spent the night with her. I suppose it set me off on the wrong track.'

'I went to her room to ask her if she'd come to London with me,' he explained, 'and I wanted to make an early start.'

'I realise that now, and I can only reiterate that I'm sorry.'

Pleased by her apology, Jay made no effort to hide it. His eyes crinkled at the corners and his mouth softened, curving back into a smile.

'Then we're friends again.' It was a statement, not a question.

'Yes.'

'Good.' He moved towards her, and she wondered if he were going to kiss her. Disappointingly, he didn't. 'Sit next to me at dinner tonight if you can,' he requested. 'And try to be kind to me during class. I've had all the bullying I can stand for one day.'

'I'd hardly call a few gentle corrections bullying,' she protested.

'Obviously you can't hear yourself. Everyone's petrified of you!'

Vicky smiled, knowing he was teasing. 'I haven't exactly noticed *you* trembling at the knees!'

'Male pride,' he shot back. 'I'm chauvinistic enough to need to prove we're still the stronger sex!' He glanced at the wall-clock. 'Still time for fifty lengths and a shower, if I hurry.'

'A cold one?'

'If you're as responsive tonight as Friday, it might not be a bad idea!'

'I see you intend to start where you left off?' she smiled.

'After a celibate weekend, what else would you suggest?'

'A celibate week, perhaps?' she parried sweetly.

Jay chuckled and moved to the door. 'As usual, you appear to have the last word!'

While trying not to read too much into Jay's conduct, Vicky could not help but be pleased that he had not gone to bed with her sister. Whether it was because he genuinely wasn't attracted to Felice, or because he was even more attracted to *her*, and sensed he might have ruined his chances by doing so, Vicky was undecided. But the mere fact that nothing untoward had happened was enough to lighten her mood and make her look on him in a different light, not only for the rest of the day, but for the week that followed.

Jay's cooking did not make any giant strides forward during that time, but he was never late for class again, and stopped playing the fool. Out of school hours he was as attentive as always, singling her out and, apart from one evening which she felt duty-bound to spend with Barry, monopolising all her free time, even the occasions she managed to snatch for a swim in the pool, when, by design or coincidence, he always happened to be there too.

But on Friday a cloud loomed on her horizon— metaphorically speaking only, for the weather, other than a couple of thunderstorms, was still unusually hot and sunny—when Jay informed her he would be going up to London for the weekend again.

'With the influx of visitors, I know you won't have time for me,' he said. 'But I'm looking forward to Tuesday when I can have you completely to myself.'

'You don't have to make excuses,' Vicky smiled, doing her best to look and sound indifferent.

One of his eyebrows lifted. 'I wasn't attempting to. But I'll reassure you all the same. I'm going for business, not sex.'

She felt herself redden, not so much at his frankness but because he was able to read her thoughts so easily.

'You certainly don't mince words,' she said aloud.

He smiled and his eyebrows rose even higher. It was a gesture she already recognised as one of his mannerisms, and an extremely attractive one too, for it gave him a faintly sardonic air.

'That's something we have in common!'

Although Vicky was determined to put Jay out of her mind during the weekend, it was easier said than done, and in spite of a hectic schedule, he was constantly in her thoughts. What was he doing . . .? Who was he seeing . . .? Had he been telling the truth . . .?

CHAPTER NINE

'WHAT happened last night? I noticed you disappearing into the garden with Jay as soon as dinner was over.'

This came from Felice on Tuesday morning as, seated in her small office, Vicky was checking some bills, setting on one side those that had to be paid immediately, and on another those that could wait.

'Nothing of any moment, if that's what you mean,' Vicky replied, looking up.

'How much longer do you intend to keep him waiting?' Felice asked curiously. 'Or have you got cold feet?'

'Of course not.'

'Then what's the problem?' The younger girl smiled winsomely. 'Tell little sister. Perhaps I can advise.'

'There is no problem,' Vicky said irritably. 'And I don't intend to give you a blow-by-blow account. You'll know soon enough when my mission's accomplished—isn't it usual to be glowing and dewy-eyed afterwards?'

'Knowing you, you'll be glowing with guilt! You're taking the whole thing far too seriously.'

'I can't help it. I'm not made the same way as you—and I don't mean that unkindly,' Vicky added apologetically.

'Am I interrupting anything?' Claudine entered the room, catching the tail end of the conversation.

'Unfortunately not,' answered Felice cryptically.

'In which case, isn't it about time you got ready? I

can see you're not made-up yet, and knowing how long
it takes you——'

'Okay, okay,' agreed Felice good-naturedly.

'I don't want to sound like a nag,' the Frenchwoman
smiled. 'But it's the first time I've given you any real
responsibility, and I'd hate you to let me down!'

'I spent most of yesterday evening making notes on
our programme,' Felice told her, 'and I supervised the
packed lunches myself. So other than the mini-bus
breaking down, there shouldn't be any problems!'

'How are *you* going to spend the day?' Vicky asked
Claudine.

'Thelma's asked me to lunch, and she's arranged a
game of bridge afterwards. I haven't played in ages, so
I pity whoever draws me as a partner!'

By the time Vicky went in to the kitchen to prepare
a picnic for herself and Jay, Felice and the other
students had departed with Claudine, who was being
dropped at Thelma's and collected on the return
journey.

Filling a basket took very little time when there
were unlimited supplies of food in the refrigerator,
and it was merely a matter of deciding the menu.

The weather, after overnight rain, was once again
more like the Mediterranean than England, and a
sundress seemed an appropriate choice. Vicky's heart
began to pound as she thought about spending a whole
day with Jay, and she experienced a sense of deep
excitement. Her hands shook as she tried to apply her
make-up, and her mascara smudged so that she had to
cleanse it off and start again. How Felice would laugh
if she could see her now, and how she would change
her mind about Vicky's cold, analytical approach to
Jay. Felice had looked stunning this morning in her
Ralph Lauren checked skirt and blouse, her copper-

coloured hair piled in loose curls on top of her head, her eyes clear and sparkling. She had had a clearly determined air about her though, as if intent on proving she was capable of acting responsibly, and Vicky hoped that today would go according to plan and that there would be no hitches. Then she put her sister out of her mind and concentrated on herself, critically eyeing her reflection and hoping her own choice of dress—sugar-pink broderie anglaise with shoe-string shoulder straps—was not too revealing. Until now, she'd only worn it on holiday. But it showed the slender lines of her body, and gave her skin the lustre of a pearl. Bolstering herself with this, she placed a slim gold bracelet around her wrist and, picking up a pink leather pochette, went downstairs.

Jay was waiting in the hall, more handsome than ever in white trousers and a grey and white flecked cotton shirt. The material clung to his wide shoulders and powerful arms, while the strong belt of muscle across his chest was clearly visible. But the muscles on his face were relaxed in a smile of greeting, his mouth teasingly quirked, in a way she would always remember him.

'As dainty and delectable as the Sugar Plum Fairy,' he commented, eyeing her approvingly. 'I feel like picking you up à la Nureyev and dancing away with you.'

Before she could reply, Eileen, one of the daily helps from a nearby village, came hurrying out of Claudine's study, duster in hand.

'There's an overseas phone call—from Hong Kong,' she said, sounding flustered and looking at Vicky. 'A gentleman. Mr——'

'That's all right,' Vicky interrupted hastily. 'It's for me. I know who it is.'

It could only be one person—George Walton.
Damn, what a shame he'd missed Claudine.

With a murmured apology to Jay, she hurried into
the room, closing the door behind her.

The line was as clear as if George were telephoning
from down the road, and quickly Vicky told him
where Claudine was, giving him Thelma's number.

'Another boy-friend?' Jay asked curiously, when
Vicky returned.

'No—a cousin.' She was annoyed to feel colour
come and go in her cheeks, as it always did when she
lied or was embarrassed.

'Does he live in Hong Kong?'

Vicky shook her head. 'He's there on—er—
business.'

'Obviously a close cousin to phone you from there,'
Jay said, slanting her a quizzical look. 'Young or old?'

'Middling.'

'What's his line?'

'Judicial robes.' Surprised at Jay's continued interest, Vicky improvised hastily. 'It's amazing the trade
they do with them in the Far East.'

'Quite amazing,' echoed Jay flatly.

'Shall we be off, then?' Vicky smiled brightly. 'We
don't want to spend all day discussing cousin ...
Walter, do we? He's sweet, but a bit of a bore.'

'I have cousins like that myself.' Jay picked up the
picnic basket from the hall table, where Vicky had left
it and, striding ahead of her, carried it out to the car.

'Which way?' he asked, as they headed down the
driveway.

'Coast or country?' Vicky enquired.

'Coast I think, if you know somewhere not too
crowded.'

'I do,' she said, thinking of the pretty village of

Medhurst, which was about an hour's run from
Beauclare's. With one pub, and a general store
doubling up as a post office, it was too small to cater
for tourists, and though she had not been there for a
few years, she was certain that unlike most other
places near the sea, time and developers would have
passed it by.

For most of the way they sped along, with only
occasional comments from Jay about the scenery.

'This dry spell is beginning to make the countryside
look more like Spain than England's green and
pleasant land,' he remarked, as they passed one
parched-looking field after another.

'Well, we've already caught the *mañana* tendency,
so who cares?' Vicky smiled.

'The farmers, probably,' replied Jay.

'I thought they wanted dry weather at this time of
the year.'

'Only when it's raining! They're the most perverse
breed—and I should know. My parents own a farm in
Kent, and their manager is the most miserable man
I've ever met. Come rain or shine, he always
grumbles!'

Vicky smiled. 'Has your father retired?'

'Yes—but he spends most of his time at the farm.
He bought it as a hobby, but he's too much of a
businessman to run it as such, and now it's self-
supporting and profitable.'

'Do you go down there often?'

'I have better things to do with my leisure hours
than tramp around pig pens, listening to my parents
discourse on the price of bacon, or grumble about
EEC subsidies. Luckily they've kept their apartment
in London, so I can see them there.'

'You really do dislike the country, don't you?' she said.

His eyes crinkled. 'It depends on which country and who I'm with!'

'How about Beauclare's and me?'

Jay chuckled. 'If you're fishing for a compliment, the answer is perfection!'

'And if I'm not?' she ventured.

'Then the answer's still perfection.' He reached across and took her hand in his large tanned one. 'You're a special kind of girl, Vicky—but then I've already told you that, haven't I?'

'I don't mind hearing it again,' she said demurely. 'Though I warn you, if you keep flattering me, it may go to my head!'

'I'll leave the champagne to do that!' His teeth gleamed as he flashed a smile. 'I put two bottles on ice early this morning, and Claudine loaned me a Freezella bag to make sure they keep cool until we're ready to drink them.'

'And I packed wine in the picnic basket,' Vicky told him. 'It looks like we're going to have quite a party!'

'But not alone, if the traffic ahead is anything to go by,' commented Jay, as with obvious reluctance he relinquished his hold on her hand, and was forced to change gear and slow down.

'That's strange,' Vicky remarked. 'According to the signpost we passed a mile or so back, we should be approaching the village.'

'Are you sure we didn't take a wrong turning?'

'Positive. I remembered the thatched-roofed pub when we turned left. They used to serve a pretty good lunch there.'

'In that case it looks as if your quiet little Medhurst has been discovered since you were last here,' Jay said, as they inched forward, and then came to a halt again. He leaned out of the window, and then turned back to Vicky. 'Get out and take a look—I think you're in for quite a shock.'

Vicky stepped out of the car, and walked over to the driving side. To her horror she saw a signpost with 'Car Park' and 'Toilets' pointing to a field already filled to overflowing. Outside stood a hot dog stand, a Coca Cola vendor, and a couple of stalls selling beach paraphernalia. Crowds of people were milling around by them as they made their way towards the beach, at least a ten-minute walk away on the far side of the village.

'The car parks nearer the beach are already full,' a voice behind informed her. 'We've already driven down there and had to turn back again.'

Vicky turned to see a young woman, dressed in shorts and halter top.

'This used to be such a quiet place,' Vicky told her.

'That must have been before the holiday camp opened,' the woman replied with a smile.

'Holiday camp?'

'Yes—some old lady with a huge house and grounds near the cliff top died, and her nephew sold it to Butler's. They've redeveloped the whole village, and now it's a kiddies' paradise.'

But not necessarily an adult's, Vicky thought to herself as she climbed back in the car.

'It's even worse than it looks from here,' she grimaced, and repeated what the young woman had told her. 'The best thing to do is turn back and see if we can find somewhere further along the coast.'

'On a day like this, in peak holiday time?' Jay's voice was sceptical. 'I've a much better idea.'

'Well, as I've made a mess of things so far, I'm prepared to listen.'

'I'd prefer it if you were prepared not to ask any questions.'

Vicky laughed. 'You can hardly keep where you're taking me a secret. I may be prepared not to ask any questions, but I can't promise not to read the signposts!'

'By then it will be too late for you to change your mind.'

With a squeal of tyres, Jay executed a U-turn, avoiding the ditch at the side of the road by inches.

'What about lunch?' Vicky asked.

'I promise you'll eat it by three—can you hold out that long?'

'I can if you can!' she smiled.

'I rarely eat lunch anyway, so it's no hardship for me.'

'Is that how you stay so slim?' she teased.

He shook his head. 'I'm one of the fortunates whose weight doesn't vary whatever they eat. Having observed you tucking in, I'd say the same thing applied.'

'It's as well. In my job I'm always testing and tasting new recipes. If I put on weight easily, I'd be as wide as I'm high!'

'Do you create, or merely copy?'

'A bit of both.'

They had reached the thatched pub, but instead of turning into one of the narrow lanes abounding, Jay cut across in the direction of the motorway.

'But that's the London road,' Vicky pointed out.

Jay touched her lips lightly with his forefinger. 'No questions, remember?'

'Yes—but——'

Her protest was silenced by music, as Jay pressed a cassette into action, and the attractive gravel-voice of Rod Stewart filled the car.

'If you don't like him, choose something else,' Jay told her. 'There's quite a varied selection. Now relax, and leave yourself in my capable hands.'

But it was not easy to relax with Jay so close beside her, his lean fingers moving the gear lever, and occasionally brushing against her thigh. But as the car hungrily ate up the miles, she found a strange peace in being near him, and was so comfortable that there was no need to make conversation, even if it had been possible above the sound of the music, which he kept in constant play. His taste ranged from Grieg to Gershwin, but there was also pop, as a complete contrast.

This man was no conformer to any rules, Vicky thought, and felt a tingle of excitement as she imagined his lovemaking. Would he be forceful, brutal, or merely sensual? Or perhaps a combination of all three. Of one thing she had no doubt: he would be a considerate lover, one who would want to satisfy his partner as much as himself. It would be a matter of pride, if nothing else, for whatever Jay did, he had to do well.

Lost in erotic fantasising, she barely noticed the houses flashing by as they left the fields of the countryside behind them, and entered the environs of London. Only when Jay stopped at their first traffic light in more than an hour and a half was she aroused from her reverie sufficiently to pay attention to her surroundings.

'Chiswick,' she said, noticing a sign.

'That's right,' Jay said cheerfully. 'We've made it in

record time. In another twenty minutes we'll be at my apartment.'

'Your apartment?' Vicky gasped in surprise. 'That's crazy!'

'Where did you think I was taking you to eat our picnic? Hyde Park?'

'I—I hadn't thought much beyond reaching London.'

'You wanted somewhere away from the crowds, didn't you? And I guarantee my flat is an absolute haven of peace and quiet.'

'It's a far cry from a tour of the local countryside,' Vicky said drily.

'But one you don't really object to?'

It was a statement as much as a question, and one Vicky had no reply to. Although she hadn't guessed he was taking her to his home, she'd been well aware of their destination, and so happy to be alone with him, she'd not really cared where they ended up.

'Won't your staff think your sudden return rather odd?' she asked.

'It's their day off—that's why I chose to come back here.'

'You mean we're going to be alone?'

'No more alone than we would have been in the quiet cove in Medhurst,' he pointed out smoothly. 'And I can assure you I won't attempt anything in my apartment I wouldn't have done there.'

'I don't necessarily find that thought particularly comforting!'

'You're not really scared, are you, Vicky?' Jay switched on his left-hand indicator and slowed into the side of the road. 'If you are, I'd be quite happy to take you somewhere else,' he said, as he came to a stop, and turned to face her. 'This has to be something we both want.'

'I assume you're not just referring to lunch?'

He half smiled. 'I'm sure you realised all along that wasn't all I had in mind.'

His words evoked an image that made her whole body grow warm, and she hoped he was not aware of it. But even as she thought it she realised she was being silly. What was the point of pretending any more? She'd intended to go to bed with him at some stage today, and what better place to do so than his apartment?

'I've never had a casual relationship before.'

As soon as she'd said it, Vicky wondered why. Was it because she didn't want him to think she was free and easy, that she was different from all his other girls? But then if she were really different she wouldn't be giving in to him now, would she? Damn! Her emotions were too confused to think clearly.

'It doesn't have to be casual, Vicky. It could be something lasting.'

'Lasting how long? Until you finish the course and come back here?'

'I can't give you a written guarantee on the time. I like to take things as they come, and enjoy them while they last.'

She swallowed her disappointment. What had she expected? A declaration of love? No, but a couple of little white lies to make her feel less cheap wouldn't have gone amiss. Dear God! Would she never be able to lose her inhibition about sex and love being one and the same thing?

'How right you are.' She forced the doubt from her voice. 'Live for today and let tomorrow take care of itself.'

Wordlessly he set the car in motion. Vicky had not expected any reaction to her acquiescence and, true to form, he had given none. He'd probably taken it for granted anyway, seeing her resistance as token, though perhaps slightly above par for the course!

'Will you tell Barry you've been to bed with me?' Jay's question took her by surprise.

'Do you disclose all *your* extra-curricular activities to your girl-friends?' Vicky asked sweetly.

His chuckle was deep and amused. 'Touché,' he acknowledged, slowing down outside a large, marble-faced block of ultra-modern apartments overlooking St James's Park, and making a left turn into an underground garage.

He drove into a parking bay marked with his name, and an attendant rushed around to open the car doors.

'Do you want the Ferrari washed, Mr Duncan?' the man asked as Jay stepped out.

'Good idea, Harry. Wax it, too. I won't need it again until this evening.'

The look Harry threw Vicky was a knowing one, and did little to add to her peace of mind. No doubt he had seen a succession of girls with Jay, and love in the afternoon was a fairly frequent occurrence.

Retrieving the picnic-basket from the boot, Jay took Vicky by the arm, and guided her towards the elevator.

'I'm on the tenth floor,' he said, and pressed the button marked 'penthouse'.

Well, at least I'm going to lose my virginity in style, Vicky thought with a smile.

'May I share the joke?' he queried.

'I was thinking of the attendant's face as we drove in,' she fibbed, though only by a couple of minutes! 'I had the feeling he'd seen it all before.'

'Considering I've lived here for five years, it would be rather peculiar if you were the first girl I'd ever brought back to my apartment!' he replied.

'True—but it would be nice to be given the impression I *was*.'

Jay looked at her, his grey eyes puzzled. 'I can't fathom you out, Vicky. One minute you act like a woman of experience, and the next like a virgin being led to the sacrificial altar. You knew the score when you agreed to come out with me today,' he reiterated. 'It was bound to end like this. It's what we both want, isn't it?'

The lift door glided open, saving the need to reply. Vicky stepped out and found herself in the marble-lined entrance hall of Jay's de luxe penthouse.

Used to large rooms at Beauclare's, she was nevertheless struck by the feeling of space, due only in part to the open planning. Two steps, inlaid with granite and brass, led down to the main reception room, which looked out on to an exquisitely land-scaped terrace, the size of a garden in the average suburban semi.

'I'll show you round later,' Jay said. 'After we've eaten.'

It's one way of manoeuvring me into the bedroom, Vicky thought, then chided herself for being so naïve. A man of Jay's sophistication would have no need for subterfuge. The suggestion would come openly and naturally. After all, today was nothing special for him, just another conquest.

'You left the champagne in the boot,' she said aloud. 'Though as far as I'm concerned, I'm happy with the wine in there.' She indicated the picnic basket.

'I didn't forget,' Jay answered. 'I always have champagne on ice in the flat.'

'Like a Boy Scout, you're always prepared!'

'I keep it for my own enjoyment, not anyone else's,' he answered coolly.

It was strange, Vicky mused, that considering he'd brought her here to take her to bed, his behaviour was not a little more agreeable. His attitude, if anything, was almost aggressive—as if what he was doing was somehow against his will. But that was ridiculous, wasn't it, given the way he'd chased her from the beginning? Could it just be he was disappointed he had caught her so easily in the end?

'I won't be long. I'll just put all this stuff on some plates.' Jay was speaking again.

'I'll help,' she volunteered.

'Thanks, but I can manage. If you want the cloakroom, there's one through that door over there.'

Deciding to take the hint, and prettify herself in preparation for their lovemaking now, rather than later, Vicky entered a luxuriously appointed room. It was fabric-lined in blue and white chintz that matched the festoon blinds at the windows, and the laminated plastic surrounding the gold-tapped vanity unit was reproduced in exactly the same pattern.

When she re-entered the living-room, Jay was in the process of transferring the contents of a laden trolley on to a glass table in front of one of the long, low silk couches. Smoked salmon pâté, lobster salad, perfectly ripened Brie, crisp warm French bread, and a bowl of seedless grapes intermingled with rosy, sun-ripened peaches. A bottle of Dom Perignon, chilled so that a bloom lay upon it, stood next to two brimming Waterford champagne glasses.

'You're not as helpless as you pretend,' Vicky commented, sitting down, and picking up a crisply laundered linen serviette.

'My cooking might not be up to much, but I wait table to perfection!'

'In an amateur capacity only, I assume?'

'I'm not averse to helping out in my restaurants, if any of them are short-handed when I'm there.' He began to eat. 'I don't believe in demarcation lines. All our executives have to be Jacks of all trades, and I expect the rest of our workforce to follow their example.'

'Don't you run into union trouble that way?' she asked, spreading her bread with pâté.

'I don't employ union labour—though I pay over union rates to my staff. It's the best way of ensuring their loyalty.'

'I thought the recession was doing that anyway.'

'I don't believe in taking advantage of it, though.' Jay sipped his champagne. 'I may be a dyed-in-the-wool capitalist, but I also have a social conscience.'

'You mean guilt at having so much money, don't you?'

He digested this remark along with the remainder of his pâté.

'Perhaps,' he agreed finally. 'Though I've never thought of it that way before.'

'I didn't mean it as a criticism,' Vicky assured him. 'Most men in your position wouldn't give a damn either way.'

'You appear to have a poor opinion of big business.'

'Like you, I'm a dyed-in-the-wool capitalist, but I happen to think small is more beautiful—certainly it's less corrupt. Some of the multi-national conglomerates are as powerful as governments, and they use that power for their own ends.'

'I agree. But if you live in a democracy, and believe in the free enterprise system, you have to take the good with the bad. There's no such thing as the perfect system, because basically people themselves are so imperfect. Governments can legislate to their hearts' content, but they can't *enforce* laws about decency and honesty.'

'Quite a speech,' she said admiringly. 'You ought to go into politics.'

'I've occasionally thought about it,' he answered with surprising seriousness. 'And with dual nationality, I could even choose which country I might do the most good in.'

'Would you like to live permanently in Italy?' Vicky questioned.

'I don't know. When I'm there I think I would, but as soon as I get back here, I find it difficult to imagine making my home anywhere else.'

'You must be completely bilingual?'

He smiled his assent. 'But then so must you, having been brought up by Claudine.'

'Yes—but my French is a bit rusty now. We're inclined to converse in English most of the time.'

'Didn't you tell me her parents were killed by the Nazis, and that she herself was lucky to escape them?'

He sounded interested enough for Vicky to recount the whole story, and he listened attentively until she had finished.

'It sounds like a movie script,' he commented finally. 'Even the happy ending!'

'Happy endings usually end in marriage, surely?'

'That sounds like a very old-fashioned concept for a thoroughly modern miss!' Jay teased.

Vicky shrugged. 'I'm not ashamed of being old-fashioned—and anyway, I want children. They'll have enough problems to face in life without giving them the added one of a single parent.'

'Surely that isn't much of a handicap these days?'

'Not according to the up-market dailies,' she answered drily. 'But in the real world, old prejudices die hard.'

'This conversation is getting too serious for me.' Deftly he removed the plates, and placed the bowl of fruit between them. 'You'll be telling me next you don't believe in sex before marriage!'

'What a waste of Dom Perignon that would be!'

'I wouldn't begrudge it, Vicky,' he said softly. 'I won't deny I want to make love to you, but it's not *just* your looks that stimulate me. You're bright as well as beautiful.'

'Thank you,' she said demurely.

Dark eyes suddenly lightened with humour. 'Aren't you going to reciprocate the compliment?'

'Would you be too disappointed if I told you I wanted you for your body alone?' she smiled.

'Not really—most women treat me as a plaything, and refuse to see that behind this fabulous physique lies a brain equal in intelligence to theirs!'

Vicky laughed. 'Can I help it if you only go out with female chauvinist pigs!'

Jay laughed as well. 'Coffee now or later?'

'Later, I think. I don't want to ruin the effect of the champagne.'

'I hope you're not implying that you can only fancy me pickled!'

'You'd be irresistible even on Perrier water!'

Perfectly true, Vicky thought, but although the alcohol had lessened her inhibitions sufficiently to say so, it had not completely destroyed them. So that when he stood, and gently drew her into the circle of his arms, she felt herself tense.

'I do believe you're nervous,' he murmured, and

pulled back slightly to look into her face. 'There's no need to be, Vicky. I shan't do anything you don't want me to.'

Her mouth trembled, and he reached out and touched it gently with his fingers, tracing the sweet outline before pulling her close again. 'I can feel your heart beating,' he went on, his voice husky. 'How fast it's going! Like a trapped butterfly. You don't feel trapped, do you, darling?'

She managed to smile as she shook her head. 'It's just that it's the first time . . . I mean the first time with you,' she amended shakily. 'I can't help feeling——'

He did not give her the chance to finish, for his mouth came gently down on hers, his tongue exploring the inner softness, before withdrawing, as if uncertain she was ready for a deeper intimacy.

His hesitation was a total surprise, though she knew it was not because he did not want her. The quickening of his breath was a clear indication that he did.

A warm tenderness suffused her, and she placed both hands on his shoulders, then moved them up along the sinewy column of his neck. With a faint murmur he covered them with his own, then drew them down to her sides, his eyes dark and clouded, his lips moving almost imperceptibly.

'You're very desirable, and it's time to do something about it,' he said thickly. 'But not here—I want our first time to be in bed.'

The movement of his hands as they gripped her under the knees and swung her up into his arms drove everything from Vicky's mind and, closing her eyes, she rested her cheek against his shoulder, while her arms entwined his neck.

Wordlessly he mounted the black and gold lacquered spiral staircase to the bedroom, door already ajar, quilted silk bedcover turned down, festoon blinds drawn, diffusing the bright sunlight to a soft, enticing glow.

As he set her down, Vicky's first reaction was one of surprise. Not merely because the scenario seemed so well prepared, but, expecting satin sheets, mirrored ceiling, and perhaps even a water bed, she was taken aback that the décor was so ordinary. Measured by any other standards, it was anything but. Sliding doors separated sleeping, bathroom and dressing areas, all of which had skirtings of brushed aluminium. Black banding on the walls and ceiling and matching lacquered cabinets on either side of the double bed were the only touches of colour. The rest—paintwork, marble bathroom and furnishings—was all white.

For a moment Jay stood in the semi-darkness with his hands cupping her face, the silence broken only by the soft hum of the air-conditioning. He traced the outline of her cheeks, eyes, forehead, the nape of her neck, until his fingers found the shoe-string straps of her bodice. While his hands untied them he kissed her, then moved to undo her zip, so that her dress slid easily to the plush carpeted floor. Vicky wore nothing beneath the top, and instinctively moved to cover her breasts with her hands.

'So sweet, so shy, so lovely,' said Jay thickly, arresting the gesture and cupping them gently in his own much larger palms, brushing the nipples with his fingers and then with his mouth and tongue. The sensation aroused her to a tumult of emotion, and suddenly all inhibitions left her, and she was left with the feeling that standing with nothing on before Jay was the most natural and wonderful thing in the world.

Even when he began to undress she did not avert her eyes, but watched him admiringly. She had never thought of the male torso as beautiful, yet Jay's was: muscular and perfectly proportioned.

When he too was naked he held her against him so that her body moulded into his, pliant as a willow. Once more he kissed her, gently, sweetly, then picked her up and carried her to the bed, placing her against a mound of cushions, so that her silky black hair splayed around her like a raven's wings. Jay lay facing her for a moment, his eyes feasting on tip-tilted breasts whose nipples resembled the tiny buds of pink tea-roses, before pressing his face against the hollow where the two curves met, using warm, wet tongue and teeth to kindle an ecstasy of desire she had never before experienced.

Without words he guided her hand down to his inner thigh, moving her hand slowly up and down his skin.

'Hold me, love me,' he whispered against her mouth, his tongue parting her lips, filling himself with the taste of her. It was as if he could not get enough of her, wanted to devour her, kiss her until they were both exhausted, satiated.

She heard the quickening of his breath, the soft groan as his fingers, stroking, caressing, aroused new sensations. New because there was only one way to satisfy them completely, one way to go to put out the flame burning within her.

Instantly he stilled all movement to look into her face, and she guessed what he was thinking.

'Don't stop,' she whispered. 'It's wonderful . . . fantastic . . . you're the best.'

Vicky had no need to ask him what he thought. The

question was, should she admit the truth? One part of
her wanted to, so he would know he was the first. For
some reason this seemed important to her. But it
might also complicate things; it could possibly
frighten him away. Yet now, more than ever, she
wanted their relationship to continue, to flower and
develop into something deeper. Suddenly, with great
clarity, she understood why. She was in love with him.
That was why sleeping with him had seemed so right,
why all doubts and fears had left her . . . why she had
not wanted to share him with Felice . . . had been
jealous of her . . . Yet it was ridiculous. How could she
love a man she had known barely three weeks? But
then there was no time limit on falling in love, just as
there was no rhyme or reason for it either. It was a
matter of the chemistry being exactly right. If it had
been simply a matter of logic, she would have fallen
for Barry months ago.

'You know, you're something pretty special.' Jay's
voice was deep and sounded sleepy. But there was
contentment in it too.

'I'm glad to know I gave satisfaction,' she said,
doing her best to sound flip.

He did not answer, but reached out to take her hand
in his, running his fingers lightly along the palm in a
delightfully erotic way.

'How about some more champagne? I'm thirsty.'

Vicky wondered why he had changed the subject.
Could he possibly imagine her pleasure to be feigned,
and want reassurance? Surely not? His expertise was
beyond doubt, and he must know it. But Jay did not
normally make remarks without a purpose—or did
he? Come to think of it, he had puzzled her on many
occasions. Could he have been testing her in some
way? Perhaps even fallen in love with her? It would

certainly explain some of the enigmatic things he had said.

With reluctance Vicky pushed this thought aside, realising the danger of imagining emotions that might not be there, simply because she wanted them to be. Live for today, she repeated to herself, for this moment, even for the next couple of weeks, and let the future take care of itself. It was an attitude she had never possessed before, but then she'd never been in love before, and at this moment, even a fleeting affair with Jay held more appeal than a sterile lifetime with someone else.

'So am I,' Vicky answered. 'I'll go down and get it.'

He did not object, and she padded into the bathroom where she'd noticed a towelling robe. Covering herself had less to do with shyness than embarrassment at the possibility of being caught naked by one of the servants, should they return unexpectedly.

Had an interior decorator had a hand in designing the apartment? she wondered as she came down the stairs into the lounge, or was it Jay's own taste? Whatever, it was difficult to fault. Modern, but not aggressively so—like its owner—the furniture was both comfortable and practical, as well as good to look at. Deeply buttoned sofas of almost cloud-like puffiness, lacquered or transparent perspex tables, and a highly polished marble floor reflected the feeling of open space and luminosity. Splashes of vibrant colour were provided by scatter cushions, objets d'art and paintings: Chagall, Dufy, Munch, Utrillo, and her own personal favourites, a pair of Magrittes, hung in a prominent position in the centre of the main wall. Jay's personal favourites too, perhaps? Vicky had never seen so many famous names outside a gallery. Jay's own collection, or given to him by his parents?

Never one to ponder when her curiosity could be satisfied, she posed the question to Jay when she returned to the bedroom, champagne and glasses in hand.

'Half and half,' came the answer. 'My parents started collecting when they were quite young, and as I wasn't born until they were almost middle-aged, you can guess they bought them for a song—certainly by today's prices.'

'Aren't you frightened they'll be stolen?' Vicky asked, as, unconscious of how fragilely feminine she looked in Jay's capacious bathrobe, she settled cross-legged on the bed.

'Petrified,' Jay answered, handing her a brimming glass of slightly warm Dom Perignon. 'Not of them being stolen—they're insured. But because they're irreplaceable, no two pictures ever being the same. But what's the point of having beautiful things if you have to lock them away in a vault?'

'I agree,' said Vicky. 'Not that I have anything worth locking away,' she added. 'Other than a couple of thousand pounds, my parents didn't leave much of value.'

'What did your father do?' Jay asked, sipping his drink.

'He was a university lecturer.'

'So teaching runs in the family?'

'You could say that, although our callings couldn't be further apart. His subject was Classics.'

'Well, so are your recipes—unless translated by me!'

Vicky smiled, admiring Jay's quick wit. 'Do you mind?' she asked, holding her glass out to him.

'Not at all, but this stuff is meant to be savoured, not swigged, you know? It can have a devastating effect.'

'So-o-o? I'm already a fallen woman—what worse can happen to me?'

Jay refilled the glass and watched in amusement as she drained it. A tiny smile played around her lips and eyes and then became a low laugh as she looked first at Jay and then at the bottle.

'Do you think it's possible to get through half a magnum without passing out?'

'I don't intend to let you try,' he responded. 'If you want oblivion, I can think of a more pleasurable way of finding it.'

'Really?' she murmured, eyes downcast.

'Really,' he echoed, gently removing the glass from her hand and placing it with his own on the bedside table. Pushing her back against the cushions, he undid the robe and slipped her free, then, sliding down into the bed, he lay on his side and put his leg over hers. 'How's this for starters?'

For a long time nothing else existed except the wonder of exploration, as they caressed each other's bodies and learned all the secret hollows to pleasure. A fever gripped her, a fever of desire, hunger, longing. But still Jay held back and would not assuage it.

'Not yet, sweetheart,' he whispered against her mouth, breath warm as a summer breeze.

'But I want you, *want* you!' she cried, body vibrantly alive.

'In a moment,' he soothed, stroking her hair, breasts, thighs.

The moment stretched into eternity as once more he brought her to a fever pitch of excitement, until she thought neither could hold back any longer. But she was wrong, for again he calmed her on the brink, before rousing her to further heights of ecstasy, or was it agony? Her limbs felt as if they were melting, dissolving; all willpower had left her, and she was riding the crest of a wave, being carried along in its wake to the edge of the sea-shore.

'I love you, I love you,' she murmured against the hollow of the broad shoulder, her nostrils filled with the musky scent of his firm smooth skin.

'And I love you,' he whispered, rubbing his face gently against her cheek. 'Darling, darling Vicky. I want us to be like this for ever.'

The words made Vicky's heart skip a beat. Did Jay mean what he was saying or was it simply the kind of endearment he normally reserved for the aftermath of lovemaking?

'Still want more champagne?' he asked, nuzzling her ear.

'Not if you can go on providing such sweet oblivion,' she replied, low-voiced.

He gave a throaty chuckle, and moved on to his back. 'Give me a quarter of an hour to recharge my batteries and I'll see what I can do!' He snuggled into the contour of her body, gently putting his arm around her and feeling the velvet swell of her firm abdomen. 'God . . . you smell so sweet . . .'

'You too . . .' she murmured, before drowsiness turned into a tranquil unconsciousness.

CHAPTER TEN

VICKY awoke feeling slightly disorientated, and it took a few minutes to realise where she was. The room was now completely dark. What time was it? she wondered, and glanced at the luminous hands of the small gold clock on the bedside table. Nine-thirty. Heavens . . . she'd been asleep nearly four hours. But where was Jay? The place beside her was empty.

Suddenly the room was flooded by light, and she put her arms over her eyes to shield them from the painful glare. Painful because she'd had too much to drink, she thought ruefully, as she raised her head and felt it pound.

'Come on, lazybones.' Fully dressed, Jay was standing over her, skin glowing, hair still wet from the shower and curling tightly round his head.

Vicky watched him for a moment before replying, enjoying the sight of him.

'How long have *you* been awake?' she asked.

'Long enough to have prepared a romantic dinner for two,' he replied with a smile.

'Prepared a romantic dinner?' she repeated. 'What are we having—baked beans on toast by candlelight?'

His lips twitched and he bit on the lower one as if he were trying not to laugh.

'Enough of your sarcasm, young lady,' he addressed her sternly. 'Raise yourself, and come down and inspect the repast for yourself.'

'Give me ten minutes to make myself look beautiful,' she requested.

'You don't need any time for that. You're beautiful already,' he said softly, and bending down, kissed her lightly on the lips.

Thoughtfully, he'd provided a fresh robe for her—the one she'd borrowed he'd used himself and it was hanging on a hook on the back of the door—though there was an assortment of fluffy towels of all sizes too, on the rail next to the glass shower cubicle.

Tinglingly refreshed after a final cold spray, Vicky could not contain her curiosity, and opened all the mirrored cupboards, inspecting them for traces of previous girl-friends. But other than a selection of expensive perfumes, obviously provided by Jay, the bathroom was strictly masculine. Choosing an atomiser of Tomango by Leonardo, her own favourite, she liberally sprayed herself.

Dressed, she inspected her reflection. Sapphire-blue eyes luminous, cheeks still slightly flushed from sleep—or drink!—otherwise no change. The true glow was inside her—though there was a certain amount of apprehension too. In the bedroom it had been easy to be natural with Jay, to be a sophisticated miss with no regrets. But now she had to face him in the cold light of day—or rather night, she corrected, recalling the time. The realisation that she loved him was still so new, so fragile, so frightening in its implications that she was uncertain how and whether she could handle it.

But when she came downstairs, and Jay handed her a drink, she realised that her fears had been groundless. He himself was playing it cool, and she was able to follow his lead without faltering, or giving any sign of her insecurity.

'To us,' he said, holding his own glass aloft and toasting her. 'And may all our days together be as memorable as this one.'

Vicky echoed the words but did not say them, trying also to pretend that she didn't know Jay's eyes were intent upon her. He sat down opposite her, content to drink in silence, his expression enigmatic, his whole body relaxed. A man who had felt desire, not love, admiration but not affection. But at least his words had given cause for hope, something to build on, a beginning that might yet have a happy conclusion.

'I hope this isn't lethal,' she said, eyeing the pink concoction in the tall glass.

'Rasberries and champagne,' Jay told her. 'Try it, it's delicious.'

She did and it was. 'Mmm! I could become addicted to this,' she murmured appreciatively.

'I'd rather you became addicted to me,' he teased. 'That way you can have the best of both worlds!'

Her eyebrows rose. 'I know Dom Perignon's considered the best, but what makes you think you are?'

His eyebrows rose. 'I'm surprised you have to ask *that* particular question,' he answered meaningfully, his eyes looking into hers. 'But I'll admit, you're not too bad either.'

'Thanks,' she said drily. 'You make me sound like lemonade against your champagne.'

'I didn't mean to,' he laughed, and cupped his glass in his hand. 'How would Château Margaux suit instead?' He named one of the world's most expensive clarets.

'Beautifully,' Vicky smiled. 'Not that I've actually tasted any, mind you. Have you?'

He nodded. 'I keep a few bottles in my cellar to impress business guests, but if you'd like to try it, I'd be happy to open one.'

'Thanks, but I'm not keen on red wine.'

'I know. But I thought that for Château Margaux you'd make an exception.'

'I'm afraid it would be wasted on my ignorant palate.'

'No, it wouldn't—you'd appreciate it at the first sip.'

'I believe you, but I'll take a rain-check all the same. I've had far too much to drink already, and another half glass of this,' she indicated the rasberry and champagne mixture, 'will see me through our meal.'

'Are you hungry yet?' he asked.

'Starving!' Vicky answered with such force that he smiled.

'In that case, let's eat.'

Arm around her waist, he led her to the dining-room. Furnished in White Vein rattan, like the lounge, it too was designed for entertaining on a grand scale, and the place-setting for two at one end of the long glass table looked somewhat forlorn, in spite of the glorious pink and white flower arrangement in a silver bowl, and the glow of candles in Lalique holders.

'Do you dine here when you're alone as well?' Vicky asked curiously as Jay held a chair for her to be seated.

'No—in my study. But it's in the process of being decorated, and in rather a mess.'

'We could have eaten picnic-style again,' she said. 'This seems rather wasted on a snack.'

'Except we're not having a snack,' Jay contradicted. 'We're going to have a meal as good as anything served at Beauclare's.'

'Made with your own two hands, I suppose?' she said disbelievingly.

'Served with them anyway,' he quipped good-humouredly.

'Who did the preparing?'

'The *chef de la maison*. He does a bulk freeze-up once a month for emergencies, so all I had to do was choose what I wanted and put it in the microwave to defrost.'

Jay had not exaggerated his cook's prowess. Lobster bisque was followed by veal with tarragon, and for dessert, praline pancakes.

'Out of this world,' Vicky praised, as she tasted a home-made *petit four* with her coffee. 'You didn't need to come to Beauclare's, Jay. You could have taken lessons from your chef.'

For a moment he looked discomfited. 'Good cooks don't necessarily make good teachers,' he answered. 'And mine's the most temperamental beggar I've ever met.'

Vicky nodded understandingly, then glanced down at her watch. 'I hate to break up the evening, but if you don't want *me* to be temperamental tomorrow, we'd better make tracks for home.'

Jay refused her offer to help clear away the dishes, as he had refused her offer to help serve the meal.

'That's what my staff are paid to do,' he said, without a backward glance at the mess. 'And they're not exactly overworked at the moment, as you can imagine.'

'How about when you're living here? Do you entertain much?'

'At least twice a week—mostly business, though. Restaurants can be very impersonal, and I find it's easier to break the ice in the intimacy of one's own home.'

'I agree, but it's lucky not everyone thinks as you do. If it wasn't for expense-account meals, ninety-five per cent of the restaurants in the country would close down.'

It was a topic that served well for most of the return journey, with Jay recounting his experiences at famous establishments, familiar to Vicky by reputation rather than as a client. He had the true storyteller's gift of bringing his subject vividly to life, and the minutes flew by as quickly as the miles. As they neared the house they fell into a companionable silence, and Vicky was pleased to think that they could feel equally relaxed without having to think of things to say.

'I'd like not to have to compete for your time with Barry,' Jay said, as he drew up outside the front door, and turned to face her, his arm resting lightly over the back of her seat. 'I like you too much to want to share you with anyone.'

The request both surprised and pleased Vicky, but however tempting it was, she had no intention of complying. Let him compete with Barry—or imagine he was. What better way of showing him she had not fallen completely under his spell, and that if he wanted sole rights on her time, he would have to find a better reason than merely liking her too much to want to share her?

'Barry's too good a friend to drop him for a summer romance, however pleasurable,' she answered carefully.

'But not *so* good that it stopped you going to bed with me?' he pointed out.

'Don't you ever have more than one girl-friend at the time?'

'It's different for men,' he said sharply.

'I thought *that* idea went out with bustles!'

'Perhaps for most girls it did, but I had the

impression you were different.' He leaned over and tilted her face to his. 'I'm not wrong, am I, Vicky?'

His mouth came down upon hers, its touch light at first, and then, as he sensed her response, his tongue parted her lips and drained their sweetness, more demanding, more possessive. The memory of their earlier lovemaking came flooding back. A tremor went through her, and her senses began to spin out of control. Her slender arms wound about his neck, clinging to him, caressing, submitting.

'Don't tell me you feel like this with Barry,' he whispered exultantly, his hands moving to her breasts, feeling their throbbing fullness, the hard pointed nipples. 'Or any other man. You want *me*, only *me*. Admit it Vicky, *admit* it.'

'I—I——' She tried to deny it, but even as she did so his lips held her prisoner, stilling the lie before she could utter it.

'Your room or mine?' he asked huskily.

All will to resist him had gone. Not only would it be anathema to go out with another man, to have Barry touch or kiss her, it would be unfair to him as well, and she made up her mind to tell him at the first opportunity. But she would not tell Jay—for the moment anyway. He could go on wondering for a little while longer.

The occasion presented itself on Sunday, when, as previously arranged, Barry arrived with a friend for a game of tennis and a swim. After they'd finished their match, he sought out Vicky, who was alone in the kitchen—there were even more visitors than usual, and she'd offered to help Jean—putting the finishing touches to a strawberry meringue gâteau.

'What gives between you and Jay Duncan?' asked Barry without preamble. 'He's obviously the reason you've been fobbing me off for the past few weeks.'

Vicky put down the forcing bag containing the cream and turned to face him.

'I'm glad you asked, though I'd every intention of telling you today anyway. I'm in love with him, Barry,' she stated simply. 'And I think he's in love with me.'

Barry ran a large, capable hand through his fair hair, ruffling it at the front, and giving him an even more boyish air.

'*Think*?' he questioned, perplexed. 'Don't you know?'

'All the signs are there,' said Vicky with certainty. 'But he hasn't got around to realising it himself.'

And this was true. For the first time Jay had not gone to London for the weekend, and he'd made it quite clear it was because he hadn't wanted to leave her. Early Saturday morning a batch of documents and letters had arrived by special messenger from his office, and he'd been busy dictating to his secretary on the telephone for most of the morning. The rest of the day he had barely left Vicky's side, mixing with the friends and relatives of the other students who had come down to visit, and even organising and playing a game of cricket with the children. He was good with them, friendly but firm, and on a first-name basis with them all.

'So congratulations are a bit premature, then?' Barry was speaking again.

'Even though I'm sure he's in love with me, I'm not sure if marriage is what he has in mind.'

'And you'd be willing to settle for less?' asked Barry with surprise.

Vicky smiled. 'I never thought I would, but that was because I've never been in love before. Frankly, I'm so bowled over, I'd agree to anything, so long as I don't lose him.' She leaned over the table and placed a hand on his arm. 'I'm sorry, Barry. It's thoughtless of me to talk like this to you about another man.'

'I'm glad you can. At least you think of me as a good friend.' He smiled ruefully. 'Now I come to think about it, that's all I ever have been, isn't it?'

The days that followed were the happiest of Vicky's life, even though Jay had still not told her outright how he felt, or talked of the future. He was flattering, attentive and loving, and each day he grew dearer to her. She made no attempt to hide how she felt about *him*, in private at least, while somehow managing to keep a distance between them during classes, so that even if everyone guessed something was going on, it was not made embarrassingly obvious.

Naturally she had confided in Claudine and Felice, and both agreed that from Jay's behaviour it seemed that it was only a matter of time before he declared himself.

'A man like Jay is bound to be wary,' Claudine said. 'But when he finally commits himself, you can be certain it's because he's tired of playing around and wants a woman he can spend the rest of his life with.'

But there was an interruption to her happiness when Jay was summoned to the telephone at the end of class one morning, returning to say he had to leave for London immediately.

'An emergency of some kind?' enquired Vicky anxiously, taking in his ragged look.

He nodded. 'Someone's made a takeover bid for my company, and I intend to fight it.'

'Of course,' she murmured sympathetically, knowing how much his business meant to him. 'How long do you think you'll be gone?'

'I'm afraid I've no idea. But I won't spend a moment

longer away from you than I have to.'

'Don't worry. I'll make sure you catch up on everything you miss.'

'To hell with the lessons—the only thing I care about missing is time away from you,' he answered fiercely. 'Don't you know how I feel?'

Joy seeped through her. Was he finally going to say the words she'd longed to hear?

'You haven't exactly made it clear,' she answered tremulously.

'Well, I will now.' He proceeded to demonstrate in a way that set the blood pounding through her veins. 'I'm crazy about you,' he muttered. 'I have been since the first day we met.' He rubbed his cheek upon hers. 'There isn't time to say all the things I want to now, though. We'll talk properly about our future when I come back.'

'Hurry,' she whispered. 'I won't have peace of mind until you do.'

'And I certainly won't have peace of body!' he said, and hugged her to him.

Within a quarter of an hour he was gone, leaving Vicky in a state of euphoria. True, he had still not convinced her he loved her, but he had used the words 'our future', and that was enough to satisfy her for the moment.

Life seemed empty without Jay, purposeless, and whereas previously she'd been content to fill her day working, she now found her interest wavering, so that even during class her thoughts were on him.

'I think you'd better take over the administrative side until Jay comes back,' Claudine told her, when for the second time running she'd botched up a demonstration recipe by leaving out a vital ingredient.

'Sorry,' Vicky apologised. 'But I've been wondering why he hasn't phoned.'

'He's only been gone a day,' Claudine pointed out with a smile. 'And you could phone him, of course.'

'I don't want to interrupt him if he's busy.'

'You can always leave a message,' the French-woman suggested practically. 'And I don't suppose he's working day *and* night.'

'If he doesn't ring tomorrow I'll——'

'Am I interrupting anything?' It was Felice, peeping round the door of Claudine's study where they were seated. 'There's a woman to see you, Vicky. Says she's a friend of Jay's.'

'Does she know he isn't here?' asked Vicky.

'Yes—it's you she wants to talk to, though.'

Claudine stood. 'You may as well show her in here,' she said, and accompanied the younger girl out of the room, considerately leaving Vicky alone.

A couple of minutes later Felice reappeared with a tall, elegantly beautiful blonde. Slender, verging on thin, with perfect features, she was about forty, and wore an expensive silk suit with Hermès accessories. Class *and* money, Vicky thought to herself, as Felice silently withdrew.

'Hello,' Vicky smiled, and held out her hand. 'I'm Vicky Marshall.'

Pointedly ignoring Vicky's welcoming gesture, and without waiting to be asked, the woman seated herself in the armchair opposite the desk.

'And I'm Lydia Walton,' she answered coolly.

The name immediately rang a bell. It was George's wife. She recalled the face now too, for they had met briefly when she'd visited the school to see her daughter, who had been one of Vicky's favourite pupils.

'I see you remember me,' Lydia Walton commented observantly. 'But then George must have talked about me a good deal too.'

'He has mentioned you, of course.' Vicky was flummoxed. Why on earth had Lydia Walton asked to see her, and not Claudine?

'I imagine, not very flatteringly.' Cold blue eyes swept over Vicky with the detached interest of a housewife examining a side of meat at the supermarket. 'You're prettier than your picture—younger-looking, too,' she said grudgingly.

'My picture?' echoed Vicky.

'The one you gave to George. I found it by accident.'

Vicky was about to say she'd never given George a picture of herself, and why on earth should she anyway? when she remembered the one he'd taken of herself and Claudine. Slowly the penny began to drop. George had told Lydia he'd fallen in love with another woman, but not her name, and, seeing the photograph, she'd made the quite natural mistake of assuming he had fallen in love with her—natural only because most men of George's advanced years showed a penchant for young girls rather than women of their own age.

'Why have you come here?' Vicky asked, deciding to find out the reason before explaining the mistake. If she could handle the situation herself, there would be no need to worry Claudine.

'To tell you that you can forget any idea of marrying George.' The voice was a purr. 'When he finds out about you and Jay, he'll come running home to me with his tail between his legs—the poor besotted fool,' Lydia added derisively.

'What—what do you mean, find out about Jay and me?' Vicky asked shakily.

'You know perfectly well.' The sound was harsh. 'You've been sleeping with him—and I've the evidence to prove it. In case George decided to believe you if you denied it, I've left nothing to chance.' She extracted a tiny tape recorder from her handbag, and pressed the switch.

'Don't tell me you feel like this with Barry.' The voice, though slightly distorted, was unmistakably Jay's. 'Or any other man. You want *me*, only *me*. Admit it, Vicky, *admit* it.'

'I—I——'

'Your room or mine?'

Vicky felt the colour drain from her face, and had she not sat down, she would have fallen. She recalled the conversation vividly. It had taken place in Jay's car after she'd slept with him for the first time at his apartment.

'Does—does Jay know about this?' she gasped.

'*Know* about it?' Lydia gave a shrill laugh. 'He planned the whole thing! George is Jay's father's best friend, and rather than see him make a fool of himself and possibly ruin his career, he came down here with the express purpose of making you fall in love with him and showing you up for the scheming little bitch you obviously are.'

Shock seemed to suspend her in a vacuum, and had her life depended on it Vicky could not have spoken. But one thing was clear in her mind. Jay did not love her. The knowledge reverberated in her head like a cracked bell.

'Well—have you anything to say?'

Vicky shook her head. What *was* there to say to this woman? That in a few minutes her whole world had fallen apart? That her love for Jay had turned to hatred for the cruel trick he had perpetrated?

Everything had been a lie: his reason for coming to Beauclare's, his interest in her, even his lovemaking.

'How long have you known?' she managed to ask finally.

'From the day it happened in Jay's apartment. I must say I was beginning to doubt his powers. You held out a long time.'

Vicky swallowed hard. She was not an innocent, but to know Jay had discussed their lovemaking in cold blood with this woman was more than she could bear.

'What would you do if I decided to fight you, and refused to give George up?' Vicky was thinking now of Claudine, not of herself.

'Every gossip columnist in Fleet Street will have the story of George's love nest, and I'll make sure your affair is presented in the worst possible light—even if I have to make up a few things as well. If I can't be Lady Walton, wife of Sir George Walton, then no one else will be either!' she shrilled.

There was no point in telling her she'd trapped the wrong woman, thought Vicky. If she'd had any doubts on the matter, they were completely dispelled by Lydia Walton's spiteful tirade. At least this way Claudine's good name would be protected, and there'd be no need for her to give George up to save his career. By the time he returned from the Far East at the end of September, his appointment would have been confirmed, as would his knighthood, and he could then present his wife with a *fait accompli* if he chose, and divorce her with impunity.

'You seem to hold all the trump cards,' said Vicky with resigned bitterness.

'Don't be a sore loser—you're young, and there are plenty of other rich, middle-aged married men around,' Lydia said, in a voice as cool as spring water.

Vicky rose. She could not bear to be in this callous woman's company a moment longer than she had to.

'I'll see you to the door.'

For the first time Lydia smiled, though it did not reach her eyes. They remained the same ice-cold blue as before.

'There's no need to be polite—in your place *I* wouldn't.'

'That's one of the *many* differences between us,' Vicky said in her most honeyed voice.

Well, at least I had the last word, she consoled herself as she watched Lydia Walton's white Mercedes coupé disappear down the driveway. But it was a hollow victory, and short-lived, once she began to think of Jay again. How could he have behaved so despicably, and why? However close George's relationship to Jay was, surely the man was old enough to sort out his own problems, decide his own future? Jay's interference was a kind of impertinence, however well-intentioned, and was somehow out of character. Unless he'd done it for Lydia's sake. She was an exceptionally beautiful woman—sophisticated and intelligent. Could it be they had once been lovers . . . might still be . . .?

Vicky felt a sharp stab of jealousy, though it was soon replaced by a remorseless ache. Jay had gone from her life for ever, and she had to come to terms with it. She swallowed a sob. How did one come to terms with a broken heart? With shattered hopes? With a life that had lost its meaning? Tears threatened and she blinked her lids.

A good many things had been explained today, things that had puzzled her; Jay's curiosity about the fathers of her pupils, and whether they had propositioned her; his lack of interest in Felice; his interrogation when George had phoned from Hong Kong; his disbelieving attitude regarding her relationship with Barry; the puzzled looks, the unwarranted jibes.

Obviously he thought she'd been using Barry to cover up her affair with George. How he must have despised me, perhaps even despising himself at the time for finding me desirable, she thought. At least that was no act. Unlike a woman, who could feign arousal, there was no way a man could pretend. But it was small consolation, and merely showed a callous side to his nature.

Much later, after finally giving way to the tears that had been threatening, and crying as she had not cried since the death of her parents, she calmed down sufficiently to be able to recount her meeting with Lydia Walton to Claudine and Felice.

'You should have told her the truth,' Claudine said angrily. 'It's not right for you to accept responsibility for something that is no concern of yours. If Jay knew——'

'It wouldn't make any difference now. He made me fall in love with him, and I loathe him for it.'

'But supposing he really is in love with you?' Felice interposed.

Vicky gave a hollow laugh. 'As he thinks I'm a cold-blooded gold-digger, do you think that's really likely?'

'You don't always fall in love with the person of your dreams,' Felice said drily. 'I should know about that!'

Vicky shook her head. 'If it was true he'd never have given that tape to Lydia, or told her about us.'

There was a silence as the logic of her argument sank in.

'What will you do if he telephones, or comes down to see you?' Claudine asked.

'I'll decide when it happens, but I don't think he will.'

In this Vicky proved wrong. Little more than an hour later she was called to the phone by Felice, who told her Jay was on the line, sounding extremely agitated.

'Do you want me to make some excuse?' she whispered, her hand over the mouthpiece.

Vicky shook her head. 'No—I'll speak to him.'

'I'll be down at the weekend,' Jay informed her cheerfully, after she'd put the receiver to her ear and tentatively said hello.

His gall amazed her. Did he imagine she would go on as before, that she was so besotted with him that she could forgive and forget?

'Vicky, are you there, sweetheart?'

'Yes—I'm here,' she said, here voice firming.

'You sound distant—you're not annoyed with me, are you?'

Annoyed!!! My God! She thought. He certainly was a great one for understatement.

'Annoyed?' she asked sweetly. 'Why should I be?'

'Because I didn't phone sooner. But I've been so tied up with meetings ... I've even been to Cap Ferrat to see my father. He's there on holiday and I needed his signature for his voting shares.'

'You must be exhausted.'

'Not really; I thrive on challenge. When everything's going smoothly I get bored.' There was a throaty chuckle. 'You're the only exception to that rule,' he said huskily.

Vicky swallowed hard. 'You obviously haven't spoken to Lydia, Jay, or you wouldn't have said that.'

'Lydia?' His tone was suddenly sharp. 'Lydia who?'

'We're not going to play games, are we?' Vicky's voice hardened. 'You know damn well who I mean. Your co-conspirator—George's wife.'

'You mean Lydia's been down to see you,' he said flatly.

'That's right, Jay. And we had a cosy little chat.'

'The double-crossing bitch!' he said savagely. 'I could murder her for this. I told her I'd handle things.'

'Don't be annoyed with her, Jay. You should thank her for doing your dirty work for you!'

'I have to see you, talk to you—explain,' he said in a rush. 'Come up to London—I'll send a car for you.'

'There's no point, Jay. It's over—finished.' Slowly she replaced the receiver, aware even as she did so of his disembodied voice calling her name.

'You're a cool one.' Felice regarded her with veneration. 'I think you're wrong, but I can't help admiring the way you handled yourself.'

'It wasn't easy.' Vicky's voice shook.

'Unpleasant things never are—but at least now it's over.'

Yes, Vicky echoed silently. Now it's *really* over.

CHAPTER ELEVEN

A POUNDING on the front door, followed by a lengthy peal of the bell, roused Vicky from a heavy sleep. She had tossed and turned for hours before exhaustion had finally overtaken her, and now, seemingly a few minutes later, she was being woken again.

She stumbled out of bed and leaned out of the open window, which overlooked the front driveway. By the light of the full moon, Jay's red Ferrari was easily visible, as was the tall, broad figure of the man himself, standing on the steps.

'Be quiet!' she snapped angrily.

Jay stepped back a few paces and looked up. 'Come down and let me in,' he ordered roughly. 'Otherwise I'm going to break the door down!'

His tone was sufficiently agitated to warn her that his threat was not an idle one, and hastily she donned a dressing-gown and tore down the stairs.

'Luckily everyone else appears to be deaf,' she said curtly, by way of a greeting. 'How dare you come here like this in the middle of the night?'

She turned to walk away from him, but he caught hold of her arm and swung her round to face him.

'I dare because it's the only time I could spare to see you.' His voice was rough, as was his grip. 'And after I've driven half the night you'll at least have the decency to listen to me.' He pulled her none too gently in to the sitting-room, shutting the door firmly behind him, and turning the key.

'Now then,' he said, switching on the wall brackets.
'Perhaps you'll look me in the face and repeat exactly
what Lydia told you.'

'I don't want to discuss it.' Vicky threw back her
head and stared at him defiantly. 'It's a closed chapter.
I loathe you and want you out of this house.' She
wrenched free of him, and Jay stepped back as if to
indicate he was not going to hold her again.

'Won't you at least give me the benefit of defending
myself?'

'Defending yourself?' she echoed derisively. 'What
is there to defend? Can you deny you came here with
the express intention of making love to me? Can you
deny that everything that happened between us was
based on lies?'

'No—I can't.' His voice was bleak. 'And I can't
claim my motives were altruistic either.'

So she'd been right. There *was* something between
him and Lydia. What else could he mean? Jealousy
seared through her like a red-hot poker, snapping the
last vestige of self-control.

'I don't want to hear any more,' she cried, as he
opened his mouth to speak again. 'You're the most
despicable man I've ever met—a cheat and a liar, and
I hate you for it!'

Her hand rose and slapped hard across his cheek.
The sound echoed in the high-ceilinged room, and
louder still in the silence that suddenly came upon it as
he stared at her wordlessly. Slowly the colour ebbed
from his face, leaving it pale with anger, except for the
red imprint of her fingers where she'd hit him.

'Isn't that rather like the pot calling the kettle
black?' His voice was deep, but toneless.

'If you're referring to George——' she said.

'And Barry, and no doubt a few others I don't know about.' A sneer curled his lips. 'And you have the cheek to call *me* a cheat and a liar!' He stepped closer again, and his eyes ranged slowly over her, from softly flushed cheeks to the rapid rise and fall of her breasts, their movement causing a faint flutter of the frilly lace that half covered them. Passion had enlarged the irises of his eyes, and his jaw moved in a jerky, uncontrolled manner. 'There's only one thing a girl like you understands,' he said thickly, and giving her no chance to escape, pulled her close and pressed his mouth on hers.

She went to turn her head away from him, but he twisted his fingers through her thick, black hair, and clasped her head so tightly that there was no way of avoiding his lips.

'You're hurting! Let me go!' she managed to gasp, as he buried his head between her breasts, kissing the warm hollow between them.

Ignoring her plea, he pulled her down on the couch, his hands forcing her arms behind her back as he pressed the whole length of his body against hers.

She attempted to shift from beneath him, but the manoeuvre only served to increase their closeness, and one of his legs came between hers and roughly forced them apart. Feeling his hard, throbbing strength against her, her anger increased, and she pushed against him with all the power she could muster. But he was far too strong for her, and it felt like pushing against a rock face.

Once again he assaulted her lips, more gently this time, but no less sensually. His hands became more gentle too, no longer gripping her like bands of steel,

but caressing her body with tantalising intimacy. Her
dressing-gown had long since come apart, and her
flimsy lawn nightdress provided no protection against
the touch of his fingers and tongue, as they stroked
and cajoled her into response.

As she felt the first awakenings, she hated herself as
much as him, yet in spite of it was powerless to resist.
With one-handed expertise he removed his clothes,
while his other hand moved across her swollen breasts
in a delightful feathery movement.

Then there was nothing between them, skin upon
skin, masculine and firm, feminine and soft, moulded
into one. Inside she was liquid fire, and Jay gasped·
with pleasure as it enveloped him.

'You're magic,' he whispered, his breath hot against
her ear. 'Sheer magic! Love me, sweetheart, love
me.'

Vicky was the first to stir, to open her eyes and come
to her senses. Satiated and exhausted, as much from
fighting him as the final ecstasy, she found that it took
a good deal of effort to shift herself from under Jay's
body. But at the first sign of movement he stood.
Momentarily they just looked at each other, and then
Vicky's face suffused with colour, and she turned her
head away.

She heard the rustle of his clothes as he dressed, and
then felt the soft silk of her dressing-gown as he placed
it with surprising gentleness over her.

Then the key turned in the lock and the door closed
silently behind him. No word of apology no goodbye,
just—nothing.

As she climbed the stairs to her bedroom she at last understood how easy it was to despise someone and yet have sex with them. How your body could betray you, and supersede the logic of your mind?

Vicky examined herself in the bathrom mirror, bleakly noting the evidence of their lovemaking in her flushed skin, swollen mouth and engorged breasts. She stepped under the shower, wanting to erase the smell of him from her body, but as she slipped into a fresh nightdress and climbed back into bed, she wished with all her heart she could erase the shameful memory of what had taken place tonight—and all the days and nights since she had first set eyes on Jay—with such ease.

It was a relief when the seminar finished in the first week in August, and the pupils departed. Jay's prolonged absence caused a good deal of comment, though Claudine had done her best to explain it away as pressure of business. The unsuccessful takeover bid was widely reported, and this gave the excuse some extra credence, but there was little that could be done to disguise Vicky's lack-lustre approach in class, or her miserable appearance out of it. At least the Advanced Course, due to start a few days later, would bring fresh faces. The old ones were a constant reminder of Jay.

'I've made up my mind to marry George, if he still wants me,' Claudine announced one evening at the beginning of September.

Vicky was delighted and showed it. 'I'm so glad!' she said, jumping up from her chair and hugging her. 'What finally decided you?'

'Seeing how miserable you've been, and knowing I'm the cause of it,' she answered, surprisingly. 'At least it will be a happy ending for one of us, and your suffering won't have been entirely in vain. But I don't intend to tell him until his position's confirmed. I'm frightened he won't be able to keep it to himself.'

'I thought lawyers were the soul of discretion.'

'A lawyer in love is very much like any other man in love,' the Frenchwoman smiled wryly. 'And he's hated this hole-and-corner business far more than I have. Probably because it's the first time for him, whereas I've been through it before.'

'But you never had the urge to marry then?'

'It was a long time ago, when I was much younger, and there were children involved. Now, with George, his daughter's grown up, and there's no one who'll be hurt.'

'I'd love to be around when George tells his wife.' Vicky gave a wan smile.

'I don't think she's the type to shed any tears.'

'Only of rage, when she realises she's been fooled.' There was a lengthy pause. 'I'd rather you didn't say anything about Jay to George, if you don't mind,' said Vicky finally. 'It might have repercussions with his father, and they've been best friends for years.'

Claudine nodded understandingly. 'Whatever you want, darling.'

'Have you given any thought to the school?' Vicky asked, shifting the subject.

'Only that I won't be able to take such an active part in running it, and you'll have to take over as head.' She frowned, regarding Vicky with concern. 'But unless you have a break away from here you won't be fit to cope as my assistant next term, let alone take on more responsibility.'

'You're right,' Vicky sighed. 'I do need a change of scene.'

'Then instead of talking about it, *do* something about it—like deciding where to go and booking up tomorrow.'

Accompanied by her best friend, Vicky spent two weeks in St Tropez. The glamorous unreality of the resort, even at the tail-end of the season, was just what she needed to take her out of herself, and sunning all day and flirting and dancing all night began to make the episode with Jay seem like an illusory dream.

George Walton's appointment as a High Court judge was confirmed at the end of October, and soon afterwards he went to Buckingham Palace to receive his knighthood. As far as he was concerned, the only thing to mar the occasion was that Claudine was not at his side. But although he had already left his wife, Claudine had thought it more appropriate for his daughter Caroline to accompany him.

The hearing was set down for the fifth of April, and the wedding was to take place ten days later. Although it was still some months away, Claudine was occupied house-hunting in London, where she intended to spend most of her week.

'I thought I'd be able to divide my time more evenly,' she told Vicky. 'But it really isn't fair to George to be a part-time wife. Lydia always hated entertaining his friends and attending functions connected with his work, and I don't want to emulate her in any way. Besides, I'm interested in everything George does.'

'I can manage perfectly well,' Vicky asserted. 'But I think it might be a good idea to take on a part-time secretary/book-keeper to take care of that side of things.'

Claudine agreed. 'Obviously you can't do the work of two people, *chérie*, so do whatever you think best.'

It was not difficult to find someone to fill the post on a non-residential basis, and a middle-aged woman from Granton was soon engaged to relieve Vicky of the more tedious tasks connected with the school.

But with George's social calendar filled to overflowing, it soon became clear that Claudine would not be able to spend any time at Beauclare's, other than occasional weekends, if she wanted to fulfil all her wifely obligations.

'I don't think George realised quite what was involved,' Claudine told her. 'Not that he isn't enjoying every minute of it, of course. After me, the law is his life.'

'Do you mean you're going to retire?' asked Vicky.

'It seems the fairest thing to do all round. It'll be a wrench, but at least I'll still have the house, and even if I can only snatch a few days here and there for the next few years, when George retires this will be our home.'

Assuming the mantle of headmistress did not daunt Vicky in the least, nor did it have any detrimental effect on the school's waiting list when the story reached the newspapers. Surprisingly, the news was given wide coverage, and there was even an interview on Breakfast Television, a break in routine Vicky thoroughly enjoyed.

'You know, you're a natural in front of the cameras,' one of the producers told her afterwards over coffee. 'How would you fancy the idea of a cookery series?'

Vicky was so surprised that she wasn't quite sure

what to say. 'I'd be interested, of course, but I don't know how I'd manage to fit it in.'

'How about during the school holidays?' the man suggested helpfully. 'We can shoot the whole series in a few weeks.'

After several discusions on the format for the half-hourly programmes, it was finally decided Vicky would go into the homes of six famous people, and cook their favourite meal for them; they would then eat it and give their honest verdict.

'The viewers will be hoping you'll make a botch of it, and occasionally we'd like you to,' the producer, Don Fox, told her with a smile. 'It makes for good audience identification if you're not too perfect! They'll also be curious to see how the famous live—what their kitchens are like, and what they're like, in a normal, everyday setting.'

Filming was arranged to coincide with the spring holidays, and with a fairly hectic schedule, it was decided that she should stay in London for the duration.

'I'll be happy to put you up,' Felice volunteered. 'My new flat's super, and you can have a bedroom to yourself.'

All Felice's dreams were finally coming true. The Duncan Diners advertising campaign had been a huge success, and she had already been contracted, at a much higher salary, for the next one. She had also had an offer to appear in a new James Bond movie, which she had accepted, and with personal appearances, and top modelling spots, she barely had a moment to breathe.

'I'd like that,' accepted Vicky gratefully. 'The television company have offered to put me up at the

Portman, but I think I'd find a hotel bedroom—however luxurious—a bit depressing for four weeks.'

'Only if you go back to it on your own,' Felice smiled. 'How is your love-life, by the way?'

'Non-existent,' Vicky smiled back. 'Barry wanted to start seeing me again, but I told him it was pointless.'

'I often see Jay,' her sister said, 'and he never fails to ask after you—talks about you a good deal, as it happens. He was really pleased when I told him about the television series.'

At the mention of Jay's name, the love Vicky felt for him washed over her again with renewed force, making a mockery of the idea that she was beginning to forget him.

'If you've any ideas of bringing us together again . . .' she threatened.

'It had occurred to me,' Felice admitted.

'Well, forget it,' said Vicky sharply.

'All right. But you'll be seeing him at the wedding, you know, so you'd better prepare yourself.'

But that was easier said than done, and as the happy day aproached, Vicky grew gradually more depressed. Yet, short of genuine illness, there was no way she could avoid seeing him, and then, realistically, she knew she would not miss Claudine's wedding if she had to be carried there on a hospital stretcher.

To give herself a lift she decided to buy an extravagantly expensive new outfit. The advance she had received from the television company, plus her increased salary as headmistress, meant that within reason money was no object and, taking Felice's advice, she headed for her sister's favourite shop in South Molton Street. She chose a side-buttoning black and cherry polka-dotted silk suit, with skating-skirt peplum, tightly belted at the waist in black patent leather. The long, slightly puffed sleeves and narrow skirt emphasised her slenderness, while the colour gave her skin the iridescent glow of a pearl.

'You look every inch a celebrity,' Felice said, without the slightest trace of envy. 'And that black and white straw boater is the perfect finishing touch.'

'I'd intended to get my hair restyled, and not wear a hat,' Vicky smiled. 'But with the re-take at Mick Miller's,' she named a world-famous pop idol, 'I didn't have time.'

The ceremony itself was at Marylebone Town Hall, but only close friends and family were invited. The remaining guests were going straight to the reception at the Hyde Park Hotel. Vicky knew Jay and his parents were among the former, and she steeled herself for their first meeting in seven months.

But it was a pointless exercise, she thought, as her heart gave a painful lurch at the first sight of him. He was formally dressed in a navy suit that made him look taller and leaner than she recalled, and though she only looked at him for a searching moment, she knew that the past months had left him totally unchanged. His tan was as bronze, his hair as black and his eyes as mocking. Only his mouth seemed different, the lips narrow as if they were held clenched all the time, and there was a hardness about his jaw that was at variance with his nonchalant manner as he greeted her.

'You look beautiful,' he said, and, fitting his step in with hers, walked towards the stairs that led to the register office.

'It's what I'm wearing,' she said nervously, over-

whelmed by his nearness and size. In the severely
formal pin-striped suit he was unlike the casually-clad
man she had last seen that fateful night at Beauclare's
when he had forced himself upon her, and it was the
memory of that time that was uppermost in her mind.

'I've never spent so much on an outfit,' she went on,
for want of something to say. 'But the money from my
television series was a bit like winning the pools, so I
thought, what the hell if I blow most of it?'

'It has nothing to do with the suit,' he said
dismissively. 'You'd look beautiful in a sack.'

Vicky felt herself growing warm. 'I was glad to read
the takeover bid was unsuccessful,' she babbled
brightly, determined to steer the conversation on to a
less personal tack. 'And I see you're expanding to the
continent as well—though not gourmet-style,' she
could not help adding.

'I'm delighted you take such an interest in my
business affairs,' he said, ignoring the barb. 'I have the
minutes of our last board meeting in my car if you'd
care to read them!' He touched her lightly on the arm.
'You never used to make polite conversation.' His
voice was deep and suddenly serious.

She tried to think of a flippant reply, but before she
could do so they arrived at the register office, where
the registrar was about to start the ceremony. All
conversation ceased, and everyone's attention focused
on George and Claudine, both of whom looked
radiant with happiness.

Afterwards, Jay introduced Vicky to his parents,
who were standing nearby. They were young-looking,
in spite of advancing years, and friendly, and it was
obvious Jay had spoken of Vicky to them.

'You're even prettier than I'd thought you'd be,' his

mother said, with a slight foreign accent that would have betrayed her Italian origin had her looks not already done so. Dark-eyed, pleasantly rounded and extremely smart, she resembled Jay in features and colouring, though he had his father's build.

'Thank you,' Vicky murmured.

'Can we give you a lift?' This was from her husband.

'That's kind of you, but I'm with my sister and we have a car.'

If Jay was disappointed he did not show it, and he disappeared shortly afterwards with his parents. Vicky breathed a sigh of relief, then remembered there was still the reception to get through. It looked like being a long afternoon!

Parking was an irritating problem as usual, and Felice drove round Harvey Nichols half a dozen times before finally deciding to take a chance and leave it on a yellow line.

'The worst that can happen is they'll tow it away,' she said carelessly and, linking her arm with Vicky's, crossed the main road to the hotel. 'At least I can well afford the fine!'

The reception was in full swing, and the smell of flowers, cigars, canapés and expensive perfume filled the air, adding to the festive atomosphere as much as the loud chattering.

After spending some time with Claudine and George, who had just presented his wife with the deeds of Beauclare's as a wedding present, Felice and Vicky split up, mingling with the guests. The majority were from George's side, Caroline, his daughter, and her fiancé, among them.

Out of the corner of her eye, Vicky spied Jay

wending in her direction, and knowing instinctively
that he had been searching for her, she excused
herself, and headed for the far side of the room where
Don Fox, the producer of her television series, had just
appeared in the entrance. They had started dating a
few weeks ago, and as coincidentally he was searching
for a weekend cottage in the area of Beauclare's, this
meant they would be able to see more of each other
than would otherwise have been possible.

'It's nice to see a face I know,' he greeted her, and
kissed her on the cheek.

'How about some champagne?' she smiled. 'It's
good and it's free!'

Don chuckled. He knew Vicky enjoyed teasing him
because he hated to pay for anything that could be
charged to his expense account.

'Like me!' he flashed. 'If only you'd give *me* the
chance to prove it!'

In spite of liking him, and finding him attractive,
Vicky had found it impossible to respond to his
embraces sufficiently to go to bed with him. Love and
sex were irrevocably intertwined in her mind, and her
affair with Jay had only confirmed this. Until she
stopped loving him, there was no way out of the
impasse. She had hoped that time would be a healer,
but if absence had not exactly made the heart grow
fonder, seeing him today had shown her that nothing
had changed.

'One day you'll get lucky,' she teased.

The small band, hired for the occasion, began to
play a waltz, and Claudine and George took to the
floor, joined after a few minutes by some of the other
guests.

'This isn't exactly my kind of music,' Don grinned, 'but how about it?'

In spite of what he'd said, he was fairly proficient, though when the tempo increased so that he could jive he was obviously happier, and performed a series of intricate steps that left her breathless.

'Funny how it's come back into fashion,' he commented, as once again the beat changed, this time to a rumba.

'Like tap-dancing,' said Vicky. 'If fashion continues to go backwards, we'll end up doing the minuet!'

'How about changing partners?' The voice was unmistakably that of Jay, who had come up behind them with Felice.

Vicky effected the introductions, and Don looked towards her questioningly.

'Do you mind?' Vicky asked him. Not that she wanted to dance with Jay, but neither did she want to make an issue of it, and she had a feeling that if she refused, he would not take no for an answer.

'Let him dare,' laughed Felice. 'He's getting the best of the deal anyway. I'm far prettier than you!'

With an immense effort of will, Vicky did not tense as Jay's arms came around her. His hands were warm about her waist, and she tried to think of them as any hands, and not the ones which had caressed her so intimately that they had brought her to an unwilling surrender. But as they began to move in time to the music, every nerve end in her body became tinglingly alive, and she longed to tear herself from his hold, ignore the pounding of her heart, and pretend she could not feel the heavy thud of his. She might not mean anything to him, but she knew he still wanted her sexually, just as much as ever.

'Why didn't you tell me the truth about George?' he asked at once. 'Why did you let me go on thinking the worst of you?'

'It didn't seem important once I'd discovered why you came to Beauclare's,' she answered coolly.

'If you loved me, the truth was very important.'

'I could say the same to you,' she retaliated.

'I'd every intention of making a clean breast of things when I came back from London. If I hadn't had to leave so hurriedly, I would have done so beforehand.'

'It's convenient for you to say so now,' she said unbendingly. 'But as I've told you, it really doesn't matter any more.'

'I don't believe you.'

For answer Vicky let her eyes move to Don. 'We're more than business friends, Jay. I thought you'd realised that.'

His jaw clenched. 'Is marriage on the agenda?' he asked stiffly.

'I'm too busy for marriage.'

'Funny, I never reckoned you for a career girl.'

'No,' she agreed. 'Like your good friend Lydia Walton, the only thing you reckoned me for was a two-timing bitch.'

She heard him catch his breath sharply, but did not wait to hear his reply. Hurrying from the floor, she made her way towards the exit, where George and Claudine were saying goodbye to some guests.

'I'm going outside for some air,' Vicky explained as she passed. 'I've a blinding headache.'

Claudine disengaged herself and came to Vicky's side. 'You look awful,' she said with concern. 'Are you sure it's just a headache?'

'Heartache as well.' Vicky forced a tremulous smile. 'Seeing Jay again was worse than I'd thought.'

'Why don't you get Don to take you home?' said the bride sympathetically. 'Or better still, somewhere bright for dinner.'

'I don't want to leave before you do.'

'You're not going to shower us with confetti, or some other such nonsense, I hope?' Claudine said with alarm. She patted Vicky's arm affectionately, to show she was teasing. 'What difference if we say *au revoir* half an hour earlier or later, *ma chère?* There's no need for that kind of formal nonsense between you and me.'

Vicky hugged her tight. 'I only hope one day I'll find a man as wonderful as George, and look as happy as you do today.'

'You already have, but you just can't see it.'

Claudine turned back to her husband, and Vicky was left wondering whether she was referring to Don or Jay.

CHAPTER TWELVE

VICKY'S television series, when it finally appeared in the early autumn, was a great success. At first it had been shown in the afternoon, but the critics' reaction was so favourable that shortly afterwards it was repeated on prime time, and a new series commissioned.

'An American TV company are putting up half the money,' Don told her excitedly, 'and they want us to shoot part of the series in the States. We have to start fairly soon, I'm afraid, so there's no way we can wait until the school holidays this time. What do you say?'

Financial aspect apart, the contract was tempting. Vicky had never been to America, and a first class, expenses-paid trip was too good a thing to turn down.

'I'll try to get someone to run the school,' she said. 'But you'll have to give me a few weeks.'

It was not a job she could advertise, for fear of rumours getting around that she was leaving on a permanent basis. But by word of mouth, through friendly contacts with other cookery establishments, a temporary replacement was found. Laurel Kingsley was thirty, and Cordon Bleu trained. She'd taught for some time at a famous London school and at an equally famous hotel in the Lake District, which specialised in residential courses.

'I was happy in both my jobs,' she told Vicky. 'But I'll have more freedom here, and frankly, more of a future. With your television career blossoming the way it is, I can see you abdicating this post permanently.'

Vicky liked her honesty, and although she had not considered giving up teaching at Beauclare's before, began to look upon it as a real possibility. She did not mention it to Claudine, though. There would be plenty of time to discuss it with her when she came back from the States, and was more certain of her own future.

Vicky left Heathrow on a cold November morning, and arrived at Miami nine hours later to be greeted by hot sunshine.

'I can't believe it!' she told Don, as they drove along the highway in their hired Buick towards the Dural Hotel, where they were spending their first night, before meeting the American TV crew the following morning.

'You will, when you're sweltering over a hot stove in Mrs Vandermowlen's kitchen the day after tomorrow, sweetie,' grinned Don, naming a famous society hostess whose husband had recently died and left an estate worth over five hundred million dollars.

But he was proved wrong. The kitchen, like the rest of the house, was air-conditioned, and if anything too cold. In size it was large enough to cater for intimate dinner parties of up to sixty, with eight double wall ovens, and three microwaves. Mrs Vandermowlen herself was enormously plump, with candy-floss blonde hair, and wore a brightly patterned silk caftan with enough gold chains and rings to give her the appearance of being a walking Fort Knox. But appearances were deceptive. There was nothing brash about her when she began to speak, nor foolish either, and she certainly knew her onions when it came to cooking!

'I started out in my folks' diner,' she confided, when

the filming was over. 'We served the best darn hash in the county.'

New York was their next stop, and the home of a writer of six hit Broadway musicals, all of which had subsequently been made into successful movies. Their base was the Plaza Hotel, situated opposite Central Park, and though the zero temperature came as a considerable shock after Florida's eighty-five degrees, it did not deter Vicky from sightseeing, or shopping.

Don had grown tired of attempting to seduce her, and their relationship had fallen into a friendly, rather than lover-like pattern, so that when he said he'd see her to the door of her room, she knew he would not attempt to go further.

If only she could have fallen for him, she thought wistfully, as he kissed her chastely on the cheek, and made his way towards the lift. He had everything to recommend him: looks, talent and integrity. What more was she looking for?

By the time the final interview was taped in Los Angeles, at the palatial home of a movie star and her equally famous director husband, Vicky was physically exhausted. An awful lot had been crammed into three weeks, and the time changes had not helped. But she still managed to enjoy the glamour and luxury of the Beverly Wilshire Hotel, and Rodeo Drive, one of the most renowned shopping streets in the world.

'I'd like to have filmed *you*,' Don told her as they boarded the plane at Los Angeles Airport for the homeward journey. 'You've been just like a little girl in fairyland.'

'Five-feet-six is hardly little,' Vicky smiled.

'I was speaking metaphorically—as if you didn't know!'

Vicky slept most of the way home, not even waking

to see the in-flight movie, a new one, that she'd intended to watch.

'I think I'm going to give up my TV career,' she said, as the taxi they were sharing drew up outside Felice's flat. 'Teaching at Beauclare's isn't anywhere near as tiring.'

'It's nowhere near as exciting either,' Don added. 'And by this time tomorrow you'll be rarin' to go again.'

'I need more than twenty-four hours to recharge *my* batteries,' she yawned.

'Well, that's all you've got, darling. There's no way I can put off the Minister of Education. Her schedule's even tighter than mine!'

By the end of January the series was complete. The tapes were being edited and the reaction was encouraging. Another series seemed almost a certainty, and with Laurel staying on, there would be no difficulty about Vicky taking time off to do it.

There were many spin-offs involved in her success, if she had had either the time or the inclination to take advantage of them. But opening shops, or lecturing to women's groups, was not her forte, though she did consent to a couple of newspaper interviews and also one with a popular magazine, for publicity purposes. The only invitation she accepted was to act as a judge in a competition to choose the Cookery Book of the Year. The prize of ten thousand pounds was being donated by a large company, who wished to remain anonymous until the winner had been chosen, and the venue for the award ceremony was to be the Inn on the Park Hotel in London.

'The panel will consist of yourself and seven other experts,' the letter had informed her, 'and among the invited guests will be the world-famous writer and gourmet, Mark Mason, who has taken a great interest in this new and exciting competition and who to launch the venture, and ensure the maximum publicity and interest, has decided to reveal his identity on the night of the presentation.'

He was a man Vicky admired enormously, enjoying his honesty and wit, while at the same time feeling slight apprehension that one man could wield so much influence, and make or break a restaurant, in much the same way certain revered theatrical critics could close a play with one bad review.

'I wonder how old he is?' Vicky was discussing the invitation with Claudine, who was down for the weekend with George.

'Fifty and probably fat,' Claudine guessed. 'Tasting all that food for a living, it stands to reason.'

'According to the papers, some people have been selling their invitations for a small fortune. It seems rather silly to buy one when it's being televised live anyway.'

'He's grown into a kind of cult figure, and I suppose the faithful want to see him in the flesh.' The grey-haired woman smiled. 'What are you going to wear for the great occasion?'

'I haven't given it a thought, though the invitation did mention something about evening dress. Do you think they mean long?'

'I doubt it, and if you haven't got anything, it seems rather a waste to buy a long dress for this one occasion,' Claudine said.

'What about the emerald green I bought in New York at Bergdorf Goodman?'

'Perfect, I'd say.'

'Does George hear anything of his ex?' Vicky took

the opportunity to ask, when George left the room to take the dog for a walk.

'Didn't I tell you? She's remarrying. I'm surprised you haven't read about it in the papers.'

'I must have missed it. Who's the lucky man? Someone well known, obviously.'

Claudine nodded. 'He has a title far more illustrious than George's! The Earl of Colchester, complete with a castle and a few million to run it—which proves the bad don't necessarily get their come-uppance!'

Vicky laughed. 'Well, at least she won't be living in London, so you won't have the embarrassment of bumping into her.'

'I assure you I wouldn't have been the least embarrassed. After the heartbreak she caused you, I'd have enjoyed the opportunity of giving her a piece of my mind!'

'She's not entirely to blame. Without Jay it could never have happened.'

'His motive still strikes me as suspect. I've a feeling there was more to it.'

'Perhaps he and Lydia had been lovers?' Vicky voiced her suspicion to Claudine for the first time.

The Frenchwoman shook her head. 'I gather from George he'd always disliked her. In fact that goes for the whole of his family.' There was a lengthy pause. 'Talking of Jay, you look terrible.'

Vicky couldn't help smiling. 'I like your thought process,' she said wryly.

'Well, it's true, *ma chère*. You're still a pretty girl, but much too thin. You must have lost over half a stone in the last eighteen months. Is it still as bad as ever?'

'It depends what you call bad. The last few days I've hardly thought of him.'

'You wouldn't . . .' Claudine hesitated. 'No, I suppose there's no point in suggesting it.'

Vicky understood all too well what she meant. 'None at all,' she said firmly. 'Everything we had to say to each other was said at your wedding.'

'Nonsense,' Claudine snorted. 'You never gave Jay the chance to explain then, any more than you did that time when he came haring down from London in the middle of the night.'

Vicky had only told Claudine that they had quarrelled again, and that Jay had left without apologising. If she guessed there was more to it, she had never said so.

'Don't forget Jay never saw the real you.' Claudine was speaking again. 'He was judging you on a totally false premise. I'm not condoning his part in the affair, but I do think you should try to look at it from his point of view as well.'

Vicky gave this some thought. 'Perhaps you're right,' she conceded finally. 'But it's too late to patch things up, even if Jay wanted to—and I'm sure he doesn't. His photograph's always in the papers with a pretty girl.'

'That's exactly it,' Claudine said impatiently. 'Always a different one. Doesn't that tell you something?'

'Only that he likes variety,' answered Vicky obdurately, and, moving to the drinks trolley to pour a pre-lunch glass of wine for them both, indicated she would like to change the subject.

But the conversation with Claudine had awakened all her memories, making it difficult for her to relax. She managed to hide her restlessness, but was relieved when the weekend passed and she could lose herself again in her work.

One week followed another, and she was glad when a couple of the staff went down with 'flu and she was put under even more pressure. This way she had no time to brood on the past or contemplate the lonely future. With Don relegated to the status of a friend, and Barry about to marry his partner, Ann, her social life, other than dates with girl-friends, was at an all-time low. It needn't have been, for there was no shortage of men locally who were interested in *her*. The trouble was, she was not interested in *them*.

The day of the competition loomed bright on her horizon. At least it would mean new faces, and, who knew, perhaps even a particular one, of more than passing interest!

One of the organisers, a suave, middle-aged man with a fixed, bright smile, greeted her at the entrance to the hotel's ballroom, and escorted her to the dais where the orchestra would normally have been, and where her co-judges were already seated. The invited audience was rapidly filling the tables, and interested glances followed her progress. But though her appearances in front of the television cameras had increased her self-confidence, she doubted if there would ever come a time when she would feel comfortable being stared at and recognised. She looked the part of a celebrity tonight though, in her emerald silk dress, a mass of fine crystal pleating, and with one shoulder bare. On this arm she wore several gold bracelets with a gold necklace encircling her throat, heavy and baroque against her translucent skin. Nervous excitement had brought a shine to her sapphire-blue eyes, and they glowed like jewels behind a barrage of thick lashes.

As introductions were effected to her co-judges, all concerned in one way or another with the world of food, Vicky smiled brightly. But not for long. At the mention of her name, a tall, broad-shouldered man who had been in deep conversation with his back to her swung round, and with a sense of shock, bordering on panic, she saw that it was Jay.

'That's Jay Duncan,' the organiser murmured as he strode towards her. 'I can tell you now that it's his company, Duncan Diners, who are sponsoring this prize.'

Had he arranged for her to be one of the judges? she wondered, or was this meeting accidental? She did not have long to wait to find out.

'Thank God you came,' he said with such obvious relief that she had her answer without doubt.

It was the first time she'd seen him in evening clothes, and though he looked as much at home in them as in more casual attire, they gave him an air of severity. But a more searching inspection told her that his change of demeanour came less from what he wore than from his looks. His skin had a greyish tinge despite its usual tan, and he appeared older, with deep lines across his forehead and a myriad of small ones fanning out from his eyes. According to the papers he was working like a demon, and if the gossip columnists were to be believed, playing like one too.

'If I'd known you were behind this, I wouldn't have come,' she said coolly, and turned to the man who had been accompanying her. But he had somehow faded from sight.

'I know, but you're here and that's all that matters.' He caught hold of her arm. 'I want to talk to you alone,' he said jerkily.

'I'm afraid I can't say the same.' Vicky tried to

wrench herself free, but his grip tightened like a vice, and short of making a scene, there was nothing she could do.

'There's thirty minutes left before the proceedings start, and I don't intend to waste a second of it,' he told her fiercely.

They were standing near the curtains hanging behind the dais, and without further ado he bundled her through them. 'I've booked a room,' he informed her, as half pulling, half dragging, he hurried her along the corridor to the lift.

If there hadn't been other people in it, Vicky would have attempted to struggle free again, but as it was there was little she could do but resign herself to hearing what he had to say.

'It's no good,' Jay said harshly, as soon as he'd closed the door of the suite behind them. 'I can't go on without you. At first I thought I could, and that time and new faces would let me forget you. But every face reminded me of you.'

'In or *out* of bed?' she flung scornfully.

'Both.' He looked at her, his eyes opaque, as if he wanted to blank out the memory. 'It's been nearly eighteen months, and I'm no saint,' he went on, his voice heavy. 'But no other woman helped, and in the end I found I didn't even want them.'

'You know what they say about having too much of a good thing,' she said, trying to appear flip though it hurt like the devil.

'You're the good thing I want, and I'll never tire of you.' His voice was so soft that she had to strain to hear it. 'Tell me you still love me. For God's sake don't let it be too late.'

At his words she began to tremble, and Jay caught her up into his arms, seeking her mouth blindly, like a man dying of hunger whose appetite craved satisfaction. She exerted all her willpower to resist him, but his touch weakened her resolve. Her hands moved along his back, stroking him, caressing him, his closeness erasing the bitterness of their separation. Time seemed to stop as they clung together, his lips enflaming her, his tongue exciting her to a fever pitch of desire. She moaned as his hands pressed against her lower back, moulding her against him as if he wished to absorb her into the very fibre of his being.

'You do love me,' he whispered. 'Don't deny it.'

'I can't,' she admitted. The sound of her own voice suddenly returned her to her senses, and she pushed herself free of him. 'But it's no use. I can't forget the past.'

'Why not? If you love me, the past no longer matters.' He reached out for her again, but she avoided him, placing the barrier of a chair between them.

'But it does. You believed I was a cheat and a liar, and didn't trust me, in spite of . . . in spite of how I'd shown my love,' she burst out.

He knew instantly what she meant. 'Don't blame me entirely for that, Vicky. When I hesitated before taking you, you denied it, and pretended your cry was passion. And even afterwards you went on pretending.'

'Only because I was scared . . . scared of losing you. That you'd guess how I really felt, and would be frightened away,' she cried. 'I thought you wanted a summer romance, not a lasting affair, and that if I could hold your interest, perhaps even make you jealous, I could prolong it, and you'd begin to want me—other than in bed.'

His hand came out and sent the chair between them

crashing to the floor. 'I wanted you for more than bed from the start. Don't you see how I was torn in two—believing you were one kind of girl because of George, while my heart told me you were another.' He gripped her shoulders so hard that it was all she could do to stop herself crying out with the pain. 'That's why I came rushing down to see you. I was going to tell you then I didn't care a damn about George, or anyone else for that matter. As long as you wanted me, and loved me as much as I loved you.'

'You certainly showed you *wanted* me,' Vicky said bitterly.

He stared at her for a moment in silence and then sighed deeply. 'I'm afraid that was guilt—guilt for my own sins, not yours. If we hadn't quarrelled, and you hadn't called me a cheat and a liar——'

'That's been the trouble with our relationship from the start,' Vicky said heavily. 'Too many ifs and buts.'

'No longer,' he vowed fiercely. 'I've got you here, and I don't intend to let you go until——'

'Mark Mason got me here,' she corrected unbendingly. 'I probably wouldn't have accepted the invitation if I hadn't been so curious to meet him.'

For the first time Jay smiled. 'You've known him for eighteen months, my darling,' he announced, enjoying her look of shocked surprise. 'We're one and the same person,' he told her, 'and we both love you more than life itself.'

It took a few moments for Vicky to recover, and even when she did she was barely able to speak.

'You mean—*you're* Mark Mason?'

'Yes, sweetheart. And I only wish I'd had the good sense to tell you so from the beginning.' His voice was deep and heavy with pain. 'When I told you that time that my motives for seducing you weren't entirely altruistic, that's what I meant. Lydia had discovered who I was, and threatened to expose me if I didn't agree to meet you and make you fall for me.'

'You mean it was all her idea?' she asked uncertainly.

He nodded. 'I refused at first. After all, I'd no right to interfere in George's life, however fond I was of him. Then she told me she knew I was Mason—she'd found a letter I'd written to George, and stolen it.' His voice was low and the words hurried, as if he couldn't get them said quickly enough. 'I know it still doesn't entirely excuse what I did, but I can only say that in those days it was important to me. That's why I decided to announce publicly tonight who I really am. It was the only way I could think of to prove I loved you, and that nothing else mattered to me any more except *you*. This cookery book prize is all part and parcel of it—to make sure you came. Vicky,' he groaned, 'I've never begged for anything in my life, but I'm begging you now. Say you forgive me.'

Recalling how he'd played her for a fool, she knew she should feel anger, but her sense of humour came to the fore, and she could only see the funny side of it.

But there was still one other thing between them, and she had to clear it from her mind.

'What about the tapes?' she asked. 'Were they Lydia's idea too?'

'I didn't even know they were in my car. She'd employed a private detective to double check on me, and that was one of his ways of doing it. I know I've behaved like a bastard, but even I would never have stooped to that,' said Jay with disgust.

With a murmur she moved towards him and rested her head on his shoulder. Through the silk of his jacket she felt the pounding of his heart as, with a convulsive movement, he wrapped his arms around her.

'There's no need to beg,' she said softly. 'I forgive you.'

'Thank God,' he said, resting his cheek on hers.

'And Mark Mason,' Vicky teased. 'If it hadn't been for him you'd never have convinced me.'

He chuckled, and drew back slightly to look into her eyes. 'How soon will you marry me?'

'Marry you?' she echoed.

'You don't think I'd settle for anything less, do you?' he said huskily and, pulling her tight against him, rained passionate kisses over her face, clasping his hands around her head, holding her neck and lightly rubbing the soft skin at her nape.

'Will next week be too soon?' he murmured. 'Don't make me wait any longer, Vicky. I may have behaved like the devil, but I've paid for it by going through hell.'

'It's not exactly been heaven for me either.' Tears shone in her eyes. 'I thought my new career would help, but it didn't, and there hasn't been another man since——'

His kiss stayed her words, and his mouth was warm and gentle. 'Do you think you need to tell me that?' he asked softly. 'In my heart I never doubted you.' His fingers wound themselves in the thick black strands of her hair, and the hardening of his limbs told her of the rising tide of his passion. 'What a lot of time we've wasted!'

Vicky pushed him away, though she still stood within the circle of his arm. 'I'm afraid we're going to have to waste some more, Jay darling. Have you forgotten about the competition?'

'I'd like to!' he said forcefully. 'But unfortunately there's no way we can.'

'We'll have a whole lifetime together,' she reminded him tenderly, 'so don't let's grudge a few hours' prize-giving.'

He gave a sigh of acceptance, and cupped her face in his hands. 'Don't leave me when it's over,' he pleaded. 'Stay with me until we can be married.'

Vicky thought of the school and the difficulties involved in suddenly handing over completely to Laurel. But they dimmed beside the longing to be with Jay, and she knew that somehow or other she would manage.

'Of course, my darling,' she agreed tremulously, and wound her arms about his neck. 'It took me a long time to win *my* prize, and I don't ever intend to be parted from it.'

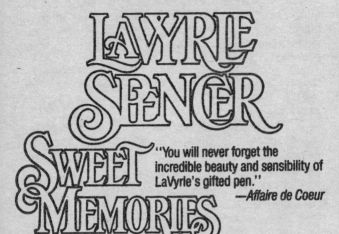

Harlequin Romance

Coming Next Month

2917 THE HEALING EFFECT Deborah Davis
Raine can't abandon young Stevie when his mother dies in the car
crash. But not until Dr. Kyle Benedict begins to show equal concern
does she think about the really eye-opening consequences of
becoming involved—with Stevie and the doctor.

2918 AN UNLIKELY COMBINATION
Anne Marie Duquette
Sherri Landers is the most competent ranger on the isolated
Colorado mountain station. And the loneliest. Until she's paired
with one M. S. Barrett, a man whose reputation for daring rescues—
and unspeakable behavior—matches her own.

2919 A STAR FOR A RING Kay Gregory
Crysten's world turns upside down when businessman Gregg
Malleson kisses her—not just because he's attractive, but because
she suddenly, disturbingly remembers where she'd met him before!

2920 MAN OF SHADOWS Kate Walker
From their first meeting Madeleine knows that Jordan Sumner is the
special man in her life. Yet how can she win his love when he is so
embittered by some secret of the past—one he refuses to even
discuss?

2921 FORTUNE'S FOOL Angela Wells
Just graduated from convent school, Ria is determined not to submit
to the arrogant Brazilian who kidnaps her on her way to join her
guardian. But Vitor Fortunato wants revenge, and he isn't going to
let this opportunity slip out of his hands....

2922 BID FOR INDEPENDENCE Yvonne Whittal
Wealthy Maura Fielding doesn't need to work, but she's determined
to be a teacher and live a normal life. She can't understand why her
stepbrother, Clayton, is so opposed. After all, she's an adult now,
free to choose.

Available in July wherever paperback books are sold, or
through Harlequin Reader Service:

In the U.S.
901 Fuhrmann Blvd.
P.O. Box 1397
Buffalo, N.Y. 14240-1397

In Canada
P.O. Box 603
Fort Erie, Ontario
L2A 5X3

COMING THIS JULY

Harlequin Historicals

*Storytelling at its best
by some of your favorite authors such as
Kristen James, Nora Roberts, Cassie Edwards*

Strong, independent heroines
Heroes you'll fall in love with
Compelling love stories

History has never been so romantic.

Look for them in July wherever Harlequin Books are sold.

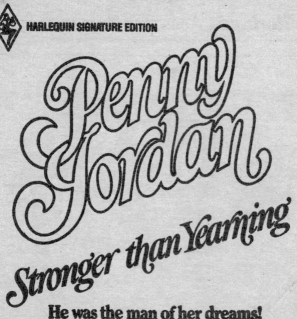

Penny Jordan

Stronger than Yearning

He was the man of her dreams!

The same dark hair, the same mocking eyes; it was as if the Regency rake of the portrait, the seducer of Jenna's dream, had come to life. Jenna, believing the last of the Deverils dead, was determined to buy the great old Yorkshire Hall—to claim it for her daughter, Lucy, and put to rest some of the painful memories of Lucy's birth. She had no way of knowing that a direct descendant of the black sheep Deveril even existed—or that James Allingham and his own powerful yearnings would disrupt her plan entirely.

Penny Jordan's first Harlequin Signature Edition *Love's Choices* was an outstanding success. Penny Jordan has written more than 40 best-selling titles—more than 4 million copies sold.

Now, be sure to buy her latest bestseller, *Stronger Than Yearning*. Available wherever paperbacks are sold—in June.

Harlequin American Romance

Romances that go one step farther...
American Romance

Realistic stories involving people you can relate to and care about.

Compelling relationships between the mature men and women of today's world.

Romances that capture the core of genuine emotions between a man and a woman.

Join us each month for four new titles wherever paperback books are sold.
Enter the world of American Romance.